EDGE OF DARKNESS

EDGE OF DARKNESS

Lynne Gessner

WALKER AND COMPANY • NEW YORK

Library of Congress Cataloging in Publication Data

Gessner, Lynne.
    Edge of darkness.

    SUMMARY: Relates the experiences of a Latvian farm
family during World War II when their country was first
subjected to Russian, then German, and again Russian
occupation.
    1. World War, 1939-1945—Latvia—Juvenile fiction.
2. Latvia—History—Russian occupation, 1940-1941—
Juvenile fiction.   3. Latvia—History—German occupation,
1941-1945—Juvenile fiction.   [1. World War, 1939-1945—
Latvia—Fiction.   2. Latvia—History—Russian occupation,
1940-1941—Fiction.   3. Latvia—History—German
occupation, 1941-1945—Fiction.   I. Title.
PZ7.G329Ed   1979   [Fic]   79-4859
ISBN 0-8027-6367-7

All the characters and events portrayed in this story are fictitious.

First published in the United States of America in 1979 by the Walker
Publishing Company, Inc.

Published simultaneously in Canada by Beaverbooks, Limited, Pickering,
Ontario.

ISBN: 0-8027-6367-7

Library of Congress Catalog Card Number: 79-4859

Printed in the United States of America

10   9   8   7   6   5   4   3   2   1

Dedicated with love to Astrida,
and to all those who remember.

To the Russians, conquering the Baltic countries gave
them access to the Baltic Sea and provided them with an
observation post from which to watch the activities of the
Germans.

To the Nazis, the Baltic countries were an easy access
into Russia, traveling over low countries to avoid the
more mountainous regions to the south.

This is the story of the period during World War II
when these two great powers fought for control.

NOTE: In Latvia all male names end with the letter *s*. In the Latvian language the *s* is dropped when speaking directly to the person—as Dāvids becomes Dāvid, Jānis becomes Jāni, Kārlis becomes Kārli.
Also Papus (Papa) becomes Papu, and Māmiņa (Mama) becomes Māmin.

Pronunciation of the major names in this story:

Dāvids	—	Dah'-vids
Jānis	—	Yah'-nis
Kārlis	—	Car'-lis
Māmiņa	—	Mah'-mi-na
Papus	—	Pah'-puss
Oskars	—	Ohs'-kars
Jēkabs	—	Yay'-kabs

CHAPTER 1

A FRANTIC WHISPER "Wake up!" came to Dāvids Ozols through the deep fog of sleep. Someone was shaking him. "Dāvid—the NKVD—they're outside!"

The NKVD—the Russian Secret Police!

Instantly awake, his heart pounding and his stomach tied in knots of cold fear, thirteen-year old Dāvids sat bolt upright, his light brown hair tumbling over his forehead.

"Are you sure?" he asked, his voice barely audible as he slid out of bed. His seven-year-old brother, Kārlis, was only a shadow standing beside him in the gloom, teeth clicking as he shivered from fear.

"Yes—I saw them," Kārlis whispered.

The big brown dog, curled on the rug between the beds, began to growl, and Dāvids reached down and clamped a hand over its muzzle. "Shut up, Stulbeni," he ordered softly. "This is no time to make noise."

They edged to the window and peeked from behind the heavy lace curtains. There in the hazy light of a Latvian

June night were three shadows moving around in the yard beyond the farmhouse.

"Bolsheviks!" Dāvids spit out the word with all the pent-up hate that Latvians feel for the Russian invaders, using the more contemptuous word *Bolshevik* instead of *Communist*, which the Russians preferred. The three shadowy forms walked over to the wagons in the yard and poked around, lifting hay to see what was underneath. Finding nothing, they headed toward the barn.

Dāvids shivered. Far into the night, his family had been celebrating the coming marriage of his sister, Daila. There had been laughing and drinking and singing; then finally his father had decided to join three of their male guests as they went out to the hayloft to sleep off their drunken stupor. They would never hear the men who were paused by the open door.

"Will they set it afire?" Kārlis whispered, pressing close to his older brother for comfort.

Dāvids made no comment. He couldn't. He was remembering the Zariņš family down the road. A little over two months before he and his mother had ridden over to visit and had just come to the edge of the woods when they saw the NKVD men. Watching fearfully, they saw the men herd the entire family into the barn—even the baby—then set the barn afire. He knew he would never forget the screams. He'd gotten sick as the roaring flames, fed by a barnful of straw and a thatched roof, had drowned out their dying cries. Māmiņa had not made a sound but had sat immobile on her horse, her face white and her blue eyes glassy with shock. When the men rode away, he had to lead Māmiņa's horse home. It was days before she recovered, and even now the horror of it was still mirrored in her eyes.

Suddenly the men turned and walked away, leaving

Dāvids shaking his head in bewilderment. Certainly there was no explaining Russian behavior. In a moment a car out front started up and sped down the lane through the pasture.

"Go back to bed, Kārli, everything's all right," Dāvids assured his brother and hugged him. Kārlis swallowed noisily, fighting back a sob, and finally crawled into his bed, pulling the sheet to his chin as though to protect himself from danger.

Dāvids crawled into his own bed, resting his hand on the dog's head. Stulbenis was kept inside at night now, because if he attacked a Russian or even barked at them when they snooped around, he would be shot. Dāvids lay staring at the window. It would be dawn in a few hours. Latvia being in a far north latitude, June days were almost eighteen hours long, and because the sun did not set very far below the horizon in the summer, the nights were not pitch dark. At the moment he yearned for the long nights of winter so he could get more rest. Eventually he calmed down and fell asleep.

Sometime later he was again abruptly awakened, this time by loud thumping. By the time his feet thudded to the floor, he realized it wasn't the threat of police—rather it was the steady oomp-pah-pah of a drum followed by music. He raced from the bedroom and peered out of the hall window to the front yard. Standing at the end of the roadway were five men playing instruments as loud as they could. The pale dawn light glowed softly on their silvery horns.

"Hey, Kārli—look—a band!" Dāvids exclaimed, coming back to shake his brother. "Come, look—a real live band!"

Groggy with sleep, Kārlis came to the hall window, rubbing knuckles in his eyes. A small, chunky boy, his blondness made him appear cherubic. After listening a minute, he pointed to an arbor of boughs interlaced with flowers that arched over the lane. "Dāvid—what's that? What's it for?"

"It's an honor gate," Dāvids replied scornfully. "For Daila and Valdis. Don't you know anything? It's traditional."

Surprise registered on Kārlis's round face. "An honor gate?"

Instantly Dāvids was sorry he'd spoken so harshly. After all, how could Kārlis know? To him life was nothing more than ugly threats, bombs, and Russians. A bride's band and an honor gate were both old Latvian customs, but because of the Russian invasion it had been a long time since a bride in these parts had had such a thing.

Suddenly the big house was astir with excitement, as all guests and the family hastily got dressed to go outside. Valdis Kalns—the scholarly looking twenty-two-year-old bridegroom—was waiting for Daila at the front door. He had been studying to be a schoolteacher, but the Russian invaders had put him to work repairing the airport near Jelgava.

"Good morning, Daila and Valdi," everyone chorused. "Today is your wedding day!" There was lots of teasing and laughing.

The two of them came down the walk arm in arm. Daila was not very tall. In fact, all the Ozolses were fairly short people and looked younger than their ages. Right now, wrapped in a pretty blue lace shawl, Daila looked more like a twelve-year-old girl on her way to a birthday party than a nineteen-year-old about to be married. Her big blue eyes held a childish look of wonder.

"Oh, Papu!" she cried when she came abreast of her father standing by the gate, grinning. "You did it!" She hugged him, then pulled away, wiping tears as she looked worriedly at him. "Oh, Papu—I know I begged for a traditional wedding—but the band—I mean all of this . . ." She waved her hand at the musician friends and the beautiful arbor.

"A man doesn't have a daughter getting married every day," Papus said, kissing her. "Walk through your gate, my lovely one."

Daila and Valdis walked through the gate and everyone cheered and clapped their hands. Despite the noise and teasing, however, there was a false note to the festivities, as though everyone was trying extra hard to create a sense of lightheartedness and joy that none of them felt. Only one week before over fifteen thousand men, women, and children—even tiny babies—had been deported in one night, destined for Siberia. Would they be next? There was never any warning.

After a while the smell of breakfast drifted out, and the group headed into the house, and soon the women were busy carrying food to the long table.

By noon everyone climbed into the wagons and headed along the dirt road toward the little white church in the village of Glūda, eight kilometers away.

After the wedding the guests returned to the big white farmhouse, and by late afternoon the long table groaned with the weight of food. Dāvids eyed it all hungrily. What he liked most was the bread. Dark sour rye bread was a staple in Latvian households, and they rarely had light bread or sweet rolls. But on special occasions all the women—guests included—vied with one another to see who could bake the lightest, the sweetest, the most delicious breads. Though Dāvids ate much of the good food, he stuffed himself on bread.

Daila and Valdis were toasted constantly, while

everyone sang and Māmiŋa's father played an accordian. Some of the guests were getting drunk, especially Oskars Mitulis. Normally Oskars rarely drank, but only ten days ago he'd broken his arm and a week before that he'd come to the house with a battered face and bruises all over his body. He sheepishly admitted he'd been drinking too much and had gotten into a fight. A quiet, almost secretive, mousy kind of man who wore glasses and smiled shyly, Oskars had been a friend of the family as long as Dāvids could remember. He was unmarried, and Dāvids knew why—he was still in love with Māmiŋa! He had dated her even before Papus came along, but he had settled for being a friend to the whole family. He was godfather to Dāvids, whom he referred to often as "the son I never had."

"A toast—a toast!" Oskars said thickly, holding onto the mantel to balance himself with one hand while he held his glass by the hand still in a sling. He waited for the music to stop. "To another lovely couple—the beautiful Elita and to Jānis—who's not so beautiful."

Everyone laughed and poked fun at Papus while their glasses clinked. It was true—Māmiŋa was still slender and pretty, and blonde like Daila and Kārlis. And today she seemed especially radiant, as the happiness of the wedding drove out all memories of Russian atrocities. Papus, on the other hand, was square-jawed and chunky, with sunstreaked brown hair, a big mustache, and hazel eyes. A white scar cut across his temple, leaving a naked path into his hair—the result of shrapnel during the war in 1917. Dāvids was proud that he looked so much like him—minus the mustache and scar, of course. To him Papus was strong. It would take an awful lot to break his spirit.

By dusk all the food on the table had been cleared

away, and the family sat in the living room, nibbling on sausage and sipping wine, talking of other weddings and happier days. Soft music came from a radio. Dāvids sat on the floor scratching Stulbenis's floppy ears while the tail beat a steady tattoo on the carpet. He wasn't a very bright dog, but Dāvids loved him. Papus had given him the dog when he was five, and they grew up together. When Dāvids was about eight, he'd fallen through ice on a nearby pond and Stulbenis had saved his life, pulling him out. Now, as Dāvids rubbed his dog's neck, he felt the hair under his hand bristle, and Stulbenis's head rose while a low growl formed in his throat.

At that moment there was a loud thump on the door—followed by another—and another. All sound inside the house ceased.

Fear sent the blood pounding to Dāvids's brain. He remembered the three men who had snooped around their place that morning. All he could think of now was—NKVD!

CHAPTER 2

NO ONE WAS ever casual about answering that kind of knock, especially with the deportations still so fresh in everyone's mind. Māmiṇa reached over and turned off the radio on a side table, then she shoved it back and put a potted plant in front of it. Why she did this, Dāvids didn't know. Many Latvians had radios. It was probably just a nervous reaction—hide everything! Meanwhile Papus walked to the door and opened it.

"Jāni Ozols—please help me," a bearded man said in Russian. Dāvids recognized the neighbor who lived at the north end of their farm.

An audible sigh of relief rippled through the room as the farmer poured forth a tale of woe in rapid Russian. Dāvids understood enough of the language to know that the farmer's cow was sick. All of the family spoke some Russian and some German.

"Speak slowly," Papus said, and the farmer began again—stating he didn't know how to cure his cow that was dying.

"I have guests—my daughter's wedding," Papus said kindly, "but I will send my hired hand." The man nodded and Papus left the room to call old Rolfs, who had often nursed the sick animals on the farm. An uneasy silence fell on the group as they stared at the bearded man clutching his hat. Māmiņa invited him to sit down, but he said no, and his eyes traveled around the room, noticing everything.

Dāvids wondered if he was snooping. Papus dealt in black market goods—something many Latvians did since the invasion. But it was considered a crime by the Russians.

Kārlis, in his usual nervous manner, began firing questions at the Russian—what was wrong with his cow?—how many children did he have?—what were their names?—how old were they?—what did he grow on his farm?—why didn't he grow rye like Papus did?—what was Russia like?—why did he leave it? The farmer looked at Kārlis with the same impatience Māmiņa often showed, and he merely mumbled a few curt replies.

Finally Papus returned with Rolfs, and the two men headed down the lane—the Russian in the lead and frail old Rolfs plodding behind.

"Papu, do you think the NKVD know about the hidden food," Dāvids asked, remembering the man's probing glance. He had not mentioned the predawn visit of the NKVD, but it had been constantly on his mind.

"The NKVD seem to know everything," Papus admitted dryly. Then he gave both sons a stern look. "But you boys must learn to be hard. Remember—if you show your fear, they know you're hiding something—that they've hit a nerve. And if they ever ask you questions—play dumb. They frequently don't know as much as they want you to think they do. Sometimes they like to scare information out of you. Keep quiet about what goes on here on this farm. Understand?"

Both boys nodded.

During the next week Dāvids worked hard alongside his father, helping with the chores. Summer was a busy time and though they had three other helpers beside Rolfs, there was always work to be done. Dāvids loved the farm and felt fiercely possessive about it. Whenever he saw the Russian farmers on their homesteads on land that had once belonged to them, he bitterly resented their intrusion.

The following Sunday Daila and Valdis came to dinner. Though normally during the week all hired hands ate in the kitchen with the family, on Sundays the family dined alone. And of course Oskars Mitulis came over, pedaling on his bicycle. Sunday wasn't Sunday without Oskars.

He walked straight into the backyard, where Papus and Dāvids worked on a broken leather harness, waiting for Māmiņa and Daila to call them into dinner. Valdis sat under the shady tree, reading a Latvian folktale to Kārlis.

"Jāni—have you heard?!" Oskars exclaimed, some inner excitement momentarily erasing his usual meek manner.

"Heard what?" Papus laid down his work and rose to shake Oskars's hand in welcome. Since handshaking was almost a ritual in Latvia, Oskars shook everyone's hand before continuing his announcement. "Germany has declared war on Russia—this morning! Their troops are marching into Lithuania." He grinned broadly as though pleased to be the bearer of such good news. "In a matter of days they'll have driven these Russian pigs out of here."

"Are you sure?" Papus exclaimed, clapping Oskars on the back. "Oh, this is the greatest news!"

During dinner the conversation was on the good news that the Russians were on the rout. "I wish I was a soldier," Dāvids said, jumping to his feet to make himself look tall.

"Don't you go getting foolish ideas," Māmiņa spoke sharply. "Your place is on this farm—not out fighting a war. Look at you—just a child. You're much too young to be involved."

Feeling deflated, Dāvids sank back into his chair. As though sensing the boy's feelings, Oskars slipped his good hand over Dāvids's smaller one. "Shame on you, Elita," he chided gently. "He's not timid—like you—and like Kārlis. He's more like Jānis—determined. You mark my word, if this boy ever wants anything bad enough, there'll be no stopping him." Oskars laughed as he gazed warmly at Dāvids. "My boy, probably not even the Russians or Germans could stop you, once you set your mind to a task. Slow you down, maybe—but not stop you." He squeezed his hand. "Remember Melnis?"

Everyone laughed. Melnis was Dāvids's black horse. Three years before he had seen the horse on another farm and was impressed with its innate good sense and keen abilities. In harness he could take a wagon where no other horse could. As a saddle horse he was without peer. Even if hitched to a plow, he performed well. And Dāvids wanted him. Papus said no, they had enough horses. For six months Dāvids persisted, breaking down every argument. He worked after hours on the farms, after putting in a full day's work on his own, to earn money for the horse. He sold his bicycle and walked the six kilometers to school to get more money. Finally the day came when he proudly rode Melnis home—his own horse. Since then, 'Remember Melnis' was the family's way of saying if Dāvids made up his mind about something, argument was useless.

The talk drifted into what they would do once the Russians were gone. "Now's the time to buy up everything we can with our rubles—to sell for German marks later on," Dāvids suggested.

"It won't be necessary," Daila assured them. "They won't do as the Russians did—leave us destitute."

Papus nodded thoughtfully. "You may be right, daughter. I certainly hope so." His brow furrowed and he stroked his mustache. "But it wouldn't hurt to buy up whatever is useful—just in case."

Shortly after dinner was over, Oskars said he wanted to return to Glūda—to hear the latest reports of the German advances. And Dāvids got his pole and headed out for his usual Sunday afternoon fishing. Kārlis didn't want to go, so he took off alone for the river a few kilometers from the farm. Because Stulbenis always splashed into the water and drove the fish away, Dāvids left him behind. As he headed along the road, he saw a familiar Russian on a bicycle. The black-haired, clean-shaven man nodded.

"Hello, Peter," Dāvids said and went on without speaking further. Peter Krekov was a man of about twenty-eight who had worked on their farm for a while. Papus had brought home this tall, broad-shouldered man one day and said he had hired him because he was a good worker. No one—not even Māmiņa—had approved.

"Jāni, I won't have one of those—those Bolsheviks on this place!" Māmiņa had yelled in anger. "Whatever made you hire him?"

Papus had shrugged and got that same look of determination that said argument was a waste of time.

"Sometimes, my dear," he had said quietly, "fate controls our actions. I need extra help while Rolfs is in the hospital, and this is what I got."

There was no disputing that. If Papus had gone to the hiring hall to find help, he would have to take whomever they assigned to him, especially since a Russian was now in charge. During the seven months Peter had been with them, he had proven to be a good worker—albeit a quiet one. No one knew a thing about him. Occasionally, both before and after he worked for the Ozols family, he was seen in Glūda, in the country store owned by Jēkabs, the Jew—probably to buy food. But where he lived, and what he did, no one knew. He seemed to have no family, no permanent home, no friends. Such a loner was always suspected, and the family—except Papus—had never accepted him or trusted him. When the longtime helper, Rolfs, had recuperated from his gall bladder operation and returned, Peter left. Today was the first time Dāvids had seen him since then, though occasionally Daila or Māmiņa reported seeing him in Glūda.

An hour after reaching the river, Dāvids had a good catch of fish on a string, and he headed home, pedaling easily along the dirt road that meandered over the rolling countryside. It would be many hours before sundown.

A rumble in the distance made him glance around. A speeding car! Only Russian soldiers drove cars in Latvia these days. He looked around quickly for a hiding place. But he was at the bottom of a long gradual hill, and there was only boggy land on each side of him. He knew every inch of the marshes around his own farm—where it was safe to step, and where not to. But these marshes were not that familiar, and a misstep could mean quicksand.

Pedaling fast, he hoped to make the top of the hill before the car came into view. There he'd be able to hide in the trees. But he was only halfway up, straining hard, when he heard it rumble across the wooden bridge over the marsh.

The car slowed down just behind him—going at a mere crawl. His heart seemed to freeze, and his hands gripped the handlebars until his fingers turned blue. His legs began to shake so badly he could scarcely pump, and the bicycle crawled agonizingly toward the top. His stomach felt as though somebody was squeezing the juices right out of it—and his chest hurt—mostly because he could hardly breathe. It was pure panic—and he couldn't hide it. That's what infuriated him—they knew he was scared! Deliberately he tried to think of hate. Just as the car came alongside him, he remembered Oskars's announcement that the Germans would drive out the Russians. They edged him into the ditch and he sprawled in the grass, tangled in his bicycle.

"You—Ozols!" came a cold steellike voice. "Get in." The man never got out of the backseat, but the one next to the driver opened the door and strode over to Dāvids, jerking him to his feet.

"I—I must take these fish home," he stammered.

The man grabbed the fish and tossed them into the brush, then he kicked the bicycle further into the ditch. Yanking open the back door, he shoved Dāvids in. The car sped off while Dāvids was still fighting to regain his balance.

"We want to ask you some questions," the man said, a definite threat in his voice.

Dāvids knew he was a prisoner of the dreaded NKVD.

CHAPTER 3

NOTHING MORE was said as the car wended its way down the dirt road, through the village of Glūda, and onto the paved road leading to Jelgava. When they passed Daila's new home, Dāvids saw his sister shaking a rug on the front porch. He wanted to yell for help, to signal her in some way. But those steely eyes, watching him as a snake watches its prey, had him so frozen in terror that he couldn't move a muscle. He'd heard about the NKVD quarters in Jelgava—the tortures that went on there, and his stomach tied up in knots from knowing that was where he was headed.

The word *torture* flashed again and again like an electric light in his brain. "You must be hard," Papus had said. But right now Dāvids felt as weak as jelly, and he folded his arms tightly to still his shaking.

Much too quickly they arrived in the big city of Jelgava, with its paved and cobblestone streets, its spired churches, its large textile and brick factories, and its sugar refineries, as well as the wide Lielupe River that flowed past it, spanned by big bridges. The narrow streets were lined with old brick or plaster buildings, and the city bustled with activity.

They drove to the huge three-story brick building that housed the NKVD headquarters for the Jelgava District, and immediately the car turned and went through open iron gates that clanged shut behind them, and they stopped behind the building.

The man in front jumped out, opened the back door of the car and jerked Dāvids out, clamping his arm tightly, and they stood waiting while the officer coolly got out and led the way inside.

On jellylike legs, Dāvids walked through an iron door, and the moment it slammed shut behind him, a scream of agony rang out from somewhere in the confines of this dark hellhole and his blood turned cold.

They walked down an endless maze of drab empty halls. The only sound was their heels clunking loudly on the stone floor. Pausing at a door, the officer knocked, and at a command from inside he opened it and shoved Dāvids in ahead of him. The room was as stark and ugly as everything else in the building, and a beefy red-faced man in uniform sat behind a desk.

"The Ozols boy," the officer said and sat down on a chair by the wall. "Son of Jānis Ozols."

The fat man nodded without looking up. "Sit down," he ordered and with a jerk of his balding head he indicated a chair by the desk. Dāvids sank into it, keeping his hands tightly closed in his lap to hide their trembling.

No one spoke. The fat man pretended to read some papers while he tapped his desk with the eraser end of a pencil—thump, thump, thump—on and on it went. Dāvids had heard how the NKVD made prisoners wait, sometimes for an hour or more, knowing that the fear, the anticipation, the absolute dread of what might happen would unnerve them. It was a form of torture itself.

He sat so still, muscles tightening, that he ached. But he was determined to "be hard," not to let them know he was afraid. He tried studying the fat man, thinking how ugly he was, comparing him to a pig, but he couldn't keep his mind on it. "What does he want?" his mind kept asking. "What're they going to do to me? Will I be killed or deported?" To himself, Dāvids sounded like Kārlis—questions piling one on top of another.

How long they sat in silence, Dāvids did not know. An hour? Ten minutes? Half a day? He tried counting the thumps, but his mind refused to function after 674.

"Your first name?" came the abrupt question from the man.

Dāvids managed to stammer his name.

"Well, Dāvid, I'm Comrade Shimkevich," he said, smiling. "Don't be afraid. We want you to answer a few questions—that's all. Then you'll be free to go home."

"Yes, sir," Dāvids squirmed uneasily. It was that friendly, purring kind of voice he hated. Behind it was always a cruel man.

"Now, Dāvid, we understand there was a lot of music at your house the other day. What was it?"

"Music?" Dāvids looked innocent.

"Yes. At dawn."

"I—I didn't hear any. I must've been asleep."

"I see. You mean you didn't hear five musicians pounding drums and blowing horns just outside your window?"

There was no use in denying it. It was obvious they had seen and heard the band. "Oh that," he answered with a shrug. "That was just to celebrate a wedding."

"Why did you lie?" The friendliness disappeared from the voice.

"I—I'd forgotten. It was a week ago."

"I want no more lies, Dāvid. Now bands cost money, don't they?"

"Money?" Dāvids asked in surprise. "Oh no, they cost us nothing. They were friends."

Ignoring the explanation, the officer continued. "Your father is very rich if he can afford a band—and much food and many guests."

Dāvids felt limp with despair. They knew everything! Vaguely he wondered if the bearded Russian farmer had spied on them and reported to the NKVD. What did they want from him now? "He saved very hard, for a long time," he said desperately, "so he could give Daila a traditional wedding."

"You lie!" Comrade Shimkevich thundered as his eyes narrowed, and inwardly Dāvids cringed, going cold, even as his hands sweated. "Tell me, where does he get his money?"

"I—I don't know." Desperately Dāvids wished he *didn't* know. "We—we sell our milk to the creamery—and some of our hay. That's all."

"Where does he get his money?" The voice was cold and demanding.

Dāvids glanced at the lean officer sitting by the wall, but there was no compassion on the cold face. "I told you," he insisted angrily, "we sell our produce—"

The man touched a bell on his desk and another burly man entered from a side door, carrying a length of rubber hose. Dāvids's throat constricted and he couldn't breathe. The burly man jerked him to his feet and held him at arm's length.

"Well?" Comrade Shimkevich demanded.

"I don't know—really I don't," Dāvids explained as casually as his pounding heart would allow. He couldn't betray Papus.

A blow of the hose caught him across the buttocks and knocked him sprawling over the desk. He felt like he'd been kicked by a horse. The pain went deep, wrenching a cry of agony from him. Somehow he managed to get to his feet again and fought to be hard as Papus had warned.

"Where?" came the demanding question again.

Some of Papus's strength seemed to flow into Dāvids and he repeated, "I don't know."

He screamed in pain when the hose struck his legs with such force that they buckled. "Are they broken?" he wondered as he crashed to the floor. His head hit the corner of the desk so hard that it sent flashes of light through his brain, and pain through his body. His tormentor jerked him to his feet and he stood swaying, while the overhead light swung in circles and the desk snaked back and forth.

"Tell me," came the demand again.

The fear of the next blow gave Dāvids strength, and he screeched defiantly, "You're wasting your time! I don't know anything. My father never tells me his business."

A hand grabbed his hair and jerked his head around so hard it felt separated from his body. Something slammed into his face—a fist probably—and he blacked out until water hit him. His lip was bleeding and so was his nose. Again he struggled to stand.

"You're very stubborn, Dāvid Ozols," Comrade Shimkevich said without feeling. "But the man beating you is strong—he doesn't wear out fast." He gave a nasty laugh. "Now—would you like to talk?"

Dāvids didn't know if he shook his head, or just stood

there—he could no longer think clearly—but another blow hit him in the stomach. For what seemed an eternity he couldn't breathe and his lungs felt on fire. Doubling over and moaning, he was terrified that he would vomit on the desk. Everything swam before his eyes and his legs turned to rubber. Once again the man yanked him up and he groped for the chair for balance. His body screamed in pain, and he heard himself moaning though he didn't want to.

"You had many guests?" came a new question. Numbly Dāvids nodded. Why lie? They already knew it. The questions came again and again—some about Papus, some about Valdis, and even some about Oskars, Māmiņa, Kārlis, and Daila. And if they didn't like his reply, the hose thudded into his agonizing body. They even asked about the Russian laborer they had hired previously. Dāvids acted dumb most of the time, trying to make his fogged brain figure out why he was here. So far they hadn't asked anything that he felt was dangerously incriminating. They already had the answers and they didn't need his. Again and again the hose slammed into his body, and he lost all track of time.

"Do you have a radio?" Comrade Shimkevich asked, switching topics again.

Dāvids remembered Māmiņa hiding it. So he merely looked dumb. Another blow of the hose to his already throbbing buttocks made him scream, and despite his resolve to say nothing, he nodded. "Yes—a radio," he mumbled, moaning as he slid limply to the floor. He was beyond fear, beyond thinking, beyond anything but the pain burning all over his tortured body. He could scarcely see. Again he was jerked up and instinctively he cringed, expecting that vicious hose.

"Where is it?" came that persistent voice.

Where was what? his fogged brain wondered. What's he talking about? Why am I here?

"You might as well talk now—because you will eventually," came the harsh voice of the fat man. "This is merely to soften you up. The real torture comes later." Dāvids groaned, too confused to know what he was supposed to say or do.

Just then a door behind him opened, and through a haze he saw Comrade Shimkevich and the other officer look up. Desperately Dāvids clung to the chair back while he fought off encroaching blackness.

"Throw the Ozols boy out. We have what we need," a voice said.

Somebody hauled Dāvids out of the door, half dragging him. In a numbing fog he stumbled down the hollow-sounding hall until finally he was shoved out into the street, but not before a fist slammed into the side of his head.

When he came to, he was in a heap on the sidewalk. People walked past, but no one looked at him or spoke. It was as though he wasn't there at all. He knew why. They were afraid.

Staggering along, he crossed a street and turned the block. Only then did he dare believe he had actually gotten out of that building alive. With the NKVD building out of sight, he sank wearily to a step, only to leap up in pain. His buttocks were like a raw boil.

Not knowing his way around Jelgava, he had no idea where to go. Despite the fog in his thinking, however, he managed eventually to find his way to the road leading to Glūda. The muscles of his buttocks were stiffening so that each step was agony, and his stomach hurt. But he was alive. He wanted to lie down and go to sleep—but he had to warn Papus. He couldn't remember why—but his one compulsion right now was to get home to Papus.

A wagon passed and he begged a ride. The woman halted and looked down at the battered, bloody boy before her as though she would take off in fear, leaving him behind. She muttered something in Russian and he groaned in despair. Why couldn't she have been Latvian instead!

"Please," he begged, "take me to my sister—first house this side of Glūda—two birch trees—front gate—pot of flowers on porch—" The fog was closing in again and his swollen lips could no longer form words.

With clucking sounds of sympathy, she climbed down and helped him into the wagon. Lying on his back hurt, so did lying on his stomach. So he settled for a side position and promptly fell into a stupor. The next thing he knew Daila and Valdis were carrying him inside their house.

"Oh, Dāvid," Daila sobbed as they laid him on their bed. "What has happened to you?"

Valdis inspected his body. "He's been beaten—probably a hose," he said angrily. "Big black bruises already on his buttocks. He won't sit down for a while. Legs are bruised—swollen—and he's been punched in the stomach—bruises under his rib cage. That *has* to be NKVD."

"Dāvid—why?" Daila said, wiping tears even as she placed a cold cloth on his swollen mouth.

"Question—Valdis—"

Though Valdis paled, he spoke calmly. "First we must get Dāvids home. Then I'll hide for a few days—until the Germans arrive."

Quickly Valdis threw some clothes in a bag, and

somehow they got Dāvids into their wagon.

He was inside his own house and on Papus's bed before he was fully conscious again, though he vaguely remembered talking in the wagon.

"He babbled all the way here," Daila was saying to Papus. "But none of it made sense—about what we did, about Kārlis in school, about the bride's band—the radio—"

"Dāvid, what did the NKVD want from you?" Papus asked urgently as he came over and sat on the edge of the bed. "Tell me, son, what specific thing did they ask? Did you tell them anything?"

Dāvids tried to remember. Why did they beat him? He couldn't think. Why was Papus questioning him? Hadn't he told him everything already? Or had he told Valdis?

"Try to think, Dāvid," Papus urged. "Try, son. I can't stay around too long . . ."

Dāvids tried to remember. The whole incident in that drab office was a blur—of hoses slamming into his body, of a fat face watching him, of words pounding in his ear. All he wanted to do was sleep. Suddenly he remembered saying they had a radio.

"I told them, Papu," he sobbed, remembering how he weakened under the torture. "I told them. I couldn't stand it any—"

Stulbenis gave a low angry growl, and seconds later three loud imperative thumps on the front door echoed hollowly in the house. As foggy as Dāvids's world was—that sound penetrated his thinking with painful clarity and he found it hard to breathe. Māmiņa paled and grabbed the bedstead, and Papus glanced around frantically as though searching for an escape. Daila sobbed as she clutched the dog's collar.

"Papu," Dāvids cried out. Somehow, though he didn't

know why, he felt he had failed his father. Had he forgotten to tell him something?

The banging came again, and Papus rose from the bed and, moving like a robot, he walked slowly out of the bedroom. In a moment they heard him open the front door.

"You have five minutes to pack a few belongings, Jāni Ozols," that steely voice said loud and clear, and Dāvids shivered, remembering the cold face, the thin lips smiling that cruel way. "You are coming with us."

A sob tore out of Māmiņa as she clutched her hands—balled into white-knuckled fists—against her breast. "Only a few more days," she moaned as Papus entered the room. "We've lived under their tyranny for over a year. Now only a few more days and they would be gone. Oh my Jānka, my husband, how cruel, how unfair!" She slumped to a chair and buried her face in her hands. "What'll happen to us? What'll happen to us?"

Papus walked over to her and tenderly touched her bowed head. Then he got a bag and began packing. Though his face was pale so the white scar into his hair stood out clearly, the square jaw was set grimly. He knew what he faced.

Even as unconsciousness slowly overcame Dāvids, one thought pierced it, bringing shame. Papus had not looked at him. He had betrayed his own father, though at the moment he couldn't remember how.

CHAPTER 4

IT WAS A GRAY, overcast day when Dāvids awoke, and for a long time he couldn't imagine why he was so sore, or even where he was. Then slowly his mind focused, and the shame in his heart drowned out the pain in his body.

"Papu!" he cried out, hoping it was all a bad dream. "Papu!"

Immediately Māmiŋa entered, followed by Oskars, who looked drawn and tired, like an old, old man.

"He hasn't come home yet," she said woodenly. Even through the fog of his thinking, Dāvids recognized the shock on her pale face. She seemed to be far away.

"How do you feel, son?" Oskars asked, gently touching his bruised face.

"Awful." Dāvids clutched his head in both hands. God, how it hurt! When he'd fallen and hit that desk, he must've bashed his brains, he thought. Or maybe the punch to his face and the clout to the head did it. Try as hard as he could to focus on one thought, the fog in his thinking interfered. He could only remember snatches

—disjointed pieces. Nor could he remember what he'd said or done. The only thing clear was the memory of that hose.

The next time he woke, Oskars was sitting beside the bed. He looked like a broken man as he reached for Dāvids with his good hand, and they mourned in silence. It seemed strange to Dāvids that Papus's death or deportation would affect Oskars so deeply. He'd always felt that Oskars's attachment to the family was to Māmiņa first, then to himself as a godchild.

True, the two men had gone hunting and fishing together, sat around a picnic campfire singing the Latvian songs together, and had generally been good friends. But he'd never realized until now how much that friendship meant to this shy, mousy man, and he felt a flood of love for him, a sharing of sorrow.

"Oskar—why did they take him?" he finally asked, wanting desperately to have him say it was a specific charge that he knew nothing about.

Oskars looked away, and guilt so filled Dāvids's mind that he cringed outwardly. Papus had known he had weakened under torture and couldn't face him. And now Oskars couldn't face him, either.

"He was my friend, Dāvid—my dear, dear friend," Oskars murmured with a catch in his voice. "Oh God, how I hate them!"

After Oskars left the room, Dāvids wallowed in his own self-loathing, wishing that the beating had taken his life. How could he face anyone—always remembering that he had broken under pressure?

When he awoke later on, Daila was sitting by the bed and he knew by the worry on her face that she hadn't heard from Valdis, who was in hiding, though Dāvids wasn't sure why.

Oskars was always around—looking exhausted. And Māmiņa—how far away she seemed!

On the following morning a sound woke Dāvids, and in panic he leaped out of bed and collapsed in a heap. The NKVD again! But finally his foggy thinking told him it wasn't a knock on the door. It was a bomb!

Struggling to stand on wobbly legs, and moaning as he moved stiff and sore muscles, he made his way to the window and clutched the sill as he stared out at smoke rising in the air. At the north end—at the part of the farm taken over by the bearded Russian—flames rose high in the air.

"Māmin?" he called out. What was going on?

Kārlis came in first, white-faced. "The Germans —they're bombing!" he exclaimed. "They've got the Bolshevik pigs on the run, Dāvid. They're bombing them right and left!"

Why would the Germans bomb a farm? Dāvids wondered. Surely from the air they didn't know each and every farm where a Russian lived. It didn't make sense.

"Are the Germans bombing us?" he asked Māmiņa in disbelief when she came into the room.

Her face was pale. "No. That was a Russian bomber." Even with the worried look on her face, she couldn't help but give a bitter smile. "He was probably aiming for Glūda—for the railroad switchyard." Dāvids nodded. It was a standing joke that a Russian bomber could never hit whatever he aimed at. Then Māmiņa went on to tell that the Germans were in fact bombing, especially wherever there was a group of Russian tanks, artillery, or soldiers as they fled toward their own country.

Dāvids crawled back into bed and hoped fervently that Comrade Shimkevich and the others at the NKVD had been wiped out—blown to smithereens.

Sometime later Oskars and Daila were talking in Dāvids's room. Evidently they thought he was asleep.

". . . rumors that some of the fleeing Soviets are slaughtering prisoners," Daila murmured, tears in her voice.

"Yes, I've heard that, too," Oskars agreed. "They're in such a hurry to get out of Latvia and the prisoners slow them down."

A sob tore out of Daila. "Do you think Papus—?"

"Oh, child, don't give yourself more misery by speculating," Oskars chided gently. "Until we know for sure—let's pray he already is on his way to Siberia."

Dāvids turned his face to the wall so they wouldn't see his tears.

"And Daila," Oskars's voice cut into his misery, "don't say anything about this to Dāvids. He's had about all he can take. And not to your mother either. She—poor dear Elita—too much has happened to her—too much horror and ugliness—and she's not the kind who can accept—"

"You mean Māmiņa is—"

"No, dear, she's not crazy. At the moment she's in shock—withdrawing from a world she can't accept. Jānis has always been her strength. That's why she chose him over me." His voice reflected wry amusement. "I'm not exactly the stalwart type, and that's what Elita needed. Give her time—she'll be all right. In the meantime, with Dāvids so battered, someone has to be strong—and I guess it falls on you."

Daila gave a sobbing laugh. "Oh Oskar, I don't *feel* very strong—"

"I know, child, I know."

Dāvids got up later on, feeling horrible, and hurting everywhere, especially his stomach. Eating was an agony, and Māmiņa fretted that maybe he had internal injuries. But by evening he felt a little better.

Oskars came over after dinner to tell that the news was all over town — the Germans were occupying Lithuania to the south and would reach the Latvian border soon. The retreating Russians were leaving a path of destruction in their wake.

While Oskars visited with Māmiņa and Daila, Dāvids went upstairs to his room because he felt unworthy to be around the family. His guilt weighed heavily on him, though he still couldn't actually remember what he'd done wrong. The whole NKVD incident was a blur — only the hose and that ironlike fist came through clear. He couldn't even remember what he'd been asked, much less what he said. Yet shortly after his release, Papus had been taken, and he was sure he had been the cause.

Downstairs, Kārlis yelled, "Where's Dāvids?"

Dāvids wasn't in the mood for his chatter, so he hobbled up the stairs to the attic. Only after he was sure Kārlis was in the kitchen again did he turn on a light. Quickly he covered the windows, though it wasn't quite dark outside yet.

Looking around at the old stuff stored in the attic, he saw things like a cradle, a high chair, broken furniture and old trunks. He remembered that in one trunk Māmiņa kept all the pictures, the outgrown clothes, and the toys of the children, and he went straight to it and opened the lid. It was as though he wanted to go back in time when everything was peaceful, when Papus was here and there was no war. He wanted to forget these past few days.

He lost all track of time, looking at pictures of when he was as young as Kārlis — a runt of a kid with wide hazel eyes and flapping ears. There was even a picture of him the day Stulbenis hauled him out of the frozen lake. Oskars had passed by just minutes after he'd been rescued, and before he took Dāvids home, shivering and ice covered, he'd taken a picture with the box camera he had with him. And poor Stulbenis, his long wet hair freezing against his gaunt body. Dāvids felt a stab of love for his loyal dog, and for Oskars who had taken off his great coat and wrapped it around him, despite the fact that under the coat Oskars had only light clothes.

When he saw the pictures of Papus, one of them where he was holding Dāvids at about age two, he quickly put the mementos away, while tears ran down his face.

"What're you doing?" came Kārlis's voice from behind. Dāvids jumped in fright and quickly slammed down the lid.

"What's the idea of sneaking up on me?" he yelled.

Kārlis backed away, startled by the attack. Then he noticed the tears. "What's wrong, Dāvid? Does your stomach still hurt? How come you're sick? What happened to you? Why doesn't somebody tell me anything? Where—?"

"Oh shut up!" Dāvids screamed at him. "How can anybody tell you anything—you never stop asking questions long enough to get an answer." He dragged a sleeve across his face to wipe the tears.

"What's in the trunk?"

"Old baby clothes."

Kārlis shrugged, not interested in baby clothes. "What's in this one?" Quickly he opened the lid of another trunk.

Lying atop some blankets that had been stored for the summer were two small leather bags. Quickly Dāvids grabbed them and opened them. Inside were rubles. So this was where Papus kept his extra money. Suddenly Dāvids remembered Papus agreeing that they should buy up whatever they could before the Germans arrived, to sell later for marks. When the Russians had invaded Latvia, they had declared all Latvian money as worthless and had substituted their own rubles. Naturally, few Latvians had rubles, so most of them were suddenly poor. But Papus had been clever—when he realized the Russian invasion of 1940 was a fact, he had bought up as much as he could of vodka, bacon, butter, honey, and cigarettes, using the Latvian money from his bank account. By the time the Russians invaded, Papus had very little money left, but every hiding place on the farm was chock full. Then he began selling these supplies whenever they were in short supply—a little at a time—to the Russians for rubles, and soon Papus had money again.

Dāvids closed the trunk lid firmly and squared his shoulders. As Oskars had said, someone here had to be strong. He couldn't afford to sit around feeling guilty any longer. Papus was gone, and he was the man of the family now. The least he could do was make up for what he'd done. And he would start by buying up supplies. That was the number-one priority.

"What're you going to do with the money?" Kārlis asked.

"We need it for supplies. Now go away and leave me alone."

Kārlis's blue eyes studied his brother. "Dāvid, how come you got hurt?"

Dāvids knew Kārlis would pester the family until someone gave him an answer. "The NKVD police beat me, because they thought I knew something about the Germans coming," he lied.

"*Did* you know anything?"

"No. Now quit bothering me."

"Where's Papus?" Kārlis persisted.

"The NKVD took him—to Siberia, we think." Dāvids swallowed the lump that rose in his throat. "And Kārli, don't ask Māmiņa any questions. She's very sad right now, because Papus is gone."

"I only wanted to know," Kārlis said in a plaintive voice, and Dāvids realized the boy had been worried, wondering about his father. After all, he no doubt heard stories, too, about the Bolsheviks. "Will he come back?" Kārlis asked, tears welling up in his eyes.

Dāvids put his hand on his brother's shoulder. "We don't know. I sure hope so. But in the meantime, you and I have to act grown up and not pester Māmiņa all the time—understand?" Kārlis nodded.

Both boys went downstairs and Dāvids didn't say anything to Māmiņa or Oskars until Kārlis went out to the barn. Then he announced, "Tomorrow I'm going to buy supplies before the Germans come." He showed them the bag of money.

Māmiņa looked alarmed. "Oh, no, Dāvid, it's much too dangerous—"

"Just living is dangerous these days," Dāvids argued. "Papus is not here to do it, so I must. We can't be caught with too little supplies."

"I know, dear," Māmiņa said placatingly. "But no one will sell to you in any quantity. You're too young."

"Then I'll convince them I'm not too young, or I'll buy in smaller quantities. But I'm going to buy up what I can." There was a firmness to his square jaw that made him resemble his father.

Stubbornness came to Māmiņa's face as she faced him. "No, you will not! I won't have you traipsing off while all this trouble is brewing. You're just a child—"

The remark cut Dāvids deeply, and his face showed his hurt, but the determination did not weaken.

"Elita, he's not a child any longer," Oskars cut in crossly. "He grew up the hard way the other night when he learned of man's brutality to man." He gave Dāvids a look of intense pride. "And I'm proud that you want to do your part. You're right—you *should* stock up." Life seemed suddenly to flow into his lined face. "I'll tell you what, Dāvid, I'll go along with you. They'll sell to the two of us. How about it?"

"Great!"

"Oh, Oskar," Māmiņa exclaimed, "that's sweet of you—but really—"

"I told you once before, when this boy makes up his mind—nothing is going to stop him. He would've gone, I could see that. Besides, I like to help him. It's the least I can do."

Dāvids knew by Oskars's last few words that he, too, needed to do something constructive. Mourning without positive action—like Māmiņa—made for a sense of helplessness.

The next morning as soon as the huge metal milk cans were filled and loaded onto the wagon, Dāvids and Oskars set out. Sitting on that hard wagon was sheer torture, but Dāvids gritted his teeth and said nothing. They rode past the little homestead that had been bombed. Only a year ago a squat, jowl-cheeked Russian officer had come, followed by about a dozen other men loaded with wooden stakes. He had announced that in compliance with the new Soviet "agrarian reform," all large farms were being divided up. The men went about driving stakes into the ground, parceling off the land until only the peat bog, the marshland, and ten hectares of decent farmland remained. Papus had been furious, and

this fine acreage had gone to the bearded Russian farmer. Their own farm was now only one-fourth of its
original size.

Dāvids felt a conflict of emotions, looking at the
gaping hole. A part of him gloated at the sight of the
burned home—it should never have been given to a
Russian. Yet he felt sadness. The bearded farmer,
though quiet and generally unsociable, had come to the
house once a long time ago and in a low voice had told
Papus, "Be careful, comrade. Do not antagonize the
NKVD. Life in Siberia is hell at any time. But life in a
Siberian slave labor camp is slow death." When Papus
had answered casually, "I have no reason to fear any
Russian," the man had added, "Go—leave Latvia while
you can. Go to Germany—anywhere—but don't stay here
to be swallowed up by my people."

Papus's face had gotten that familiar stubbornness. No
one would ever drive him from his land. And the bearded
farmer had left, never to return until the night of the
wedding. His warning had gone unheeded, and now
Papus was gone—to Siberia, to a slow death. And all that
was left of the Russian and his family was a gaping hole
in the ground.

"What happened to the family?" Dāvids asked.

"Blown to bits." There was such smug satisfaction in
Oskars's voice that Dāvids could only stare at him. This
was a tragic event, yet gentle Oskars had no compassion.
How great must be his hate!

At the creamery in Glūda they sold the milk, took the
rubles they got in payment, and added them to what they
already had. Then they drove to the distillery beyond
town. Vodka was always a good commodity to have.
People would buy it, no matter what the price.

They covered the cases of vodka with a tarp and took

the back roads home, to avoid any soldiers that might be riding by. At home they hid some of the cases of vodka in storage pits dug in the ground under the hay in the barn, and some in well-hidden pits in the big grainery building. They went out again, traveling the back trails, stopping at nearby towns at every available store, buying up a carton or two of cigarettes at each place.

Heading home, they were not too far from the farm when a wagon came toward them, driven by a wizened bearded man. It was loaded with his family and belongings. He didn't pull over but glared hatefully at Dāvids and Oskars. Instinctively Dāvids knew he was a Bolshevik, fleeing the advancing Germans.

"Get over," the man bellowed in Russian. At the moment Dāvids was driving the wagon. He could see the man was in a hurry—the Russian retreat route was fast closing. All of his own hate for the Bolsheviks boiled up in one burning flash of rage. All he could see was a fat NKVD face and a hose hitting him. It blinded him to any kind of reason.

"Get out of my way or I'll ram my wagon against yours," he yelled back. He knew if they sideswiped, they could possibly tear off the man's wheel, and he might even damage his own wagon, but thwarting this Bolshevik's escape suddenly seemed paramount. Cracking a whip over the two horses, he charged ahead on the narrow road. With a roar he snapped the whip again, urging the horses on. They bolted in surprise.

At the last moment the Russian, swearing profusely, yanked his horse aside and his wagon careened off the trail, hitting a tree before bouncing back. Dāvids turned and spit into his wagon, even as he saw some of the belongings shift and slide onto the ground.

Oskars gave a laugh of grim revenge. "That did my

soul good—seeing a Bolshevik scared," he said through clenched teeth.

Looking back at the Russian who had climbed off his wagon to retrieve his goods, they saw him shake his fist, calling out names.

Dāvids's joy knew no bounds. He had defied a Russian and spit in his wagon. He had laughed in his face. The intense satisfaction it gave him helped smother the shame he had felt from being beaten.

They drove in silence a moment, then looking straight ahead, Dāvids asked, "Do you think they've killed Papus?"

Oskars swallowed before answering. "I'd like to say no. But knowing the Bolsheviks—I'm afraid maybe they did."

"I hope so, Oskar," Dāvids murmured. "I surely hope so."

"Why?" came the startled reply.

"Because otherwise they'll torture him all the time. They actually enjoy torturing. You can't imagine what they're like—"

"Can't I, Dāvid?"

The question was asked so softly, but with such intensity of feeling that Dāvids turned to stare at him. Suddenly his glance went to the broken arm still in the sling, and he remembered the earlier battered face and bruised shoulder. Oskars had moved painfully for days, and had sheepishly brushed off questions about his injuries by saying he'd been drunk and gotten into a fight. Yet Oskars wasn't really a drinking man—not that much, anyway. And he certainly wasn't the fighting kind. It suddenly became clear to Dāvids—Oskars, too, had been dragged to the NKVD headquarters and beaten. After

all, the police would know he was a close friend of Jañis
Ozols. Yet Oskars had not betrayed his friend. It took
Jānis's own son to do that.

"Jānis saved my life once, Dāvid—did you know that?"
Oskars asked.

Dāvids forced his thoughts from his own self-
condemnation. "No—how?"

"In the other war—ran out of the trenches and hauled
me back. I'd have bled to death, otherwise. That scar he
carries—he got it then." Again came a deep sigh. "I wish
I could give my life for him—oh God, how I wish I
could! He didn't deserve to die." Then, as though aware
of the gloom that had settled over them, he looked at
Dāvids and said proudly, "He was a true patriot, my boy.
He loved Latvia. He fought to make her free once." He
put a hand on Dāvids's arm. "Don't ever forget that,
Dāvid—he fought to make Latvia free."

"I won't forget, Oskar," Dāvids said solemnly.

By the time they got home it was near dark and Dāvids
was ready to drop from exhaustion. His head pounded
and his body ached. No position was comfortable, and
despite the overcast sky, he was hot. But he felt good—at
least he had done a man's work.

Māmiņa was in the barn—milking. "All hands quit
today—all but Rolfs," she announced, looking haggard.
"They're flocking to the farms the Bolsheviks have
deserted—to claim them before the Germans get here."
She motioned for Dāvids to get down. "So pitch in and
help me get this milking done."

Wearily he slid off the wagon, while Oskars hid the
cartons of cigarettes. Before Oskars left, he promised to
find some farm help for them.

Each day there was more news of fresh German advances. The Nazi party leaders called on the ill-equipped and scattered Latvian army to come out of hiding and help defeat the Russians. They wanted Latvians to kill the Russians—burn them out!

And this was exactly what the Latvians were doing.

CHAPTER 5

TEN DAYS AFTER Dāvids was beaten, the Germans overran Latvia. It was like a holiday and the family went to Glūda to watch the Panzer unit throbbing along the road to Jelgava and Riga. Both sides of the street were lined with Latvians waving their crimson-white-crimson flags, strewing flowers along the roadway, and cheering their liberators. First came the tanks, their cleats churning up the dirt street. They looked powerful, bristling with guns, and the ground under Dāvids's feet trembled like an earthquake.

Crowding alongside these tanks were the trucks loaded with officers in green uniforms with red tabs on their collars. Their squarish helmets gleamed dully under a coating of dust. Most of them looked glum and important, but one man grinned down at Dāvids and threw him a German mark. Dāvids stuffed it in his pocket. Behind the armored division came the heavy artillery pulled by big Belgian horses, and bringing up the rear were the foot soldiers with rolled up sleeves and choking on dust. They grinned broadly when some of the young Latvian girls ran up and hugged them. Villagers yelled greetings, and the soldiers yelled joyously back.

It was impressive, Dāvids thought, watching their booted feet thump in true military precision. Though dust-covered and sweating, these Germans were not at all like the sloppy Bolsheviks when they invaded the Baltic countries a year before. Yet there was a similarity—a victorious army parading past—an army that was not their own.

He put his doubts aside and swallowed the lump in his throat when he heard the Latvian national anthem suddenly blare forth from radios set proudly in windows—a song they hadn't heard in a year. How beautiful it sounded.

"Dāvid, my boy!" a voice called out of the crowd, and Dāvids spun around to see Jēkabs, the wispy-haired, hunched Jew who owned the country store. His coat hung loosely on his tall, emaciated frame, and one brass button was missing. Dāvids and Kārlis greeted him joyously, and as usual his bony fingers shoved some hard candy into their hands.

Jēkabs stayed behind the crowd, eyeing the Germans warily.

"It's a great day, isn't it, Jēkab?" Dāvids exclaimed. "Listen—our anthem. Gives me goosebumps."

The wrinkled face creased in a smile. "Ah yes, it's a joy to hear it." He lowered his voice. "Dāvid, do you hear anything of your papa?" Dāvids shook his head. "Too bad, too bad," Jēkabs murmured. "Such a good man." He peered at Dāvids when Kārlis turned back to watch the parade. "Did you know, my boy, that your papa hid me on your farm when the Russians first came looking for Jews?"

"No, I didn't know," Dāvids admitted, remembering the commotion caused when the Bolsheviks first began deporting Jews. Many Jews were successful, wealthy businessmen, owning banks, stores, and factories. And such capitalism was an offense to the Soviet regime. For this reason they persecuted the Jews during the early stages of the invasion.

"After a while," Jēkabs continued in his barely audible voice, "when they sort of forgot about us, I returned to my store here in Glūda. But I owe my life to your kind papa."

Dāvids looked around worriedly. If such a thing was known by the wrong person, it could get the family in trouble. He wasn't surprised, however, to learn that Papus had done this. He was always helping someone. And on a farm like theirs it would be easy to hide a man.

"A good man," Jēkabs murmured again. Then he bid Dāvids good-bye and shuffled out of sight—a mere ghost of a man moving in a crowd.

Suddenly all the cheering, the excitement, was gone out of Dāvids's day. He resented Jēkabs for taking away the great feeling that they were being liberated. Seeing him hiding in the crowd made him think of Papus—who hadn't lived to see Latvia once again free.

As much as they wanted to stay and watch the unending procession, the family had to get back to the farm. Old Rolfs wasn't very strong since his gall bladder operation. Actually, about all he was good for these days was taking the cows to pasture and staying all day with them before bringing them back at night—a job that normally a child would do. Stulbenis would go along and do most of the work, keeping them from straying too far.

They piled into the wagon and headed home, across the beautiful countryside of rolling green hills wearing shawls of dark forests. Colorful meadow flowers caught the rays of the sun, which had burned a hole in the clouds overhead, and along the road edge wild strawberry plants were in bloom. The air smelled of lilacs and jasmine and warm earth. Dāvids's depression lifted—this was his land—his home. He sat up straighter on the seat, feeling very much a man.

His thoughts went back to his childhood. Until the Russian invasion a year ago, he had never known anything but freedom for his country, though freedom was something new to Māmiņa and Papus. But often he'd listened to them and Oskars talk about the days of their own childhoods when Latvia had been ruled by Russians as well as Germans. Then came the First World War, and the Latvians fought valiantly to drive out their enemy. Flashes of memory brought Dāvids clear pictures of Papus's grinning face whenever he spoke of that day in November 1918 when Latvia finally became free. How proud he was of that!

And a surge of deep-seated emotion brought tears to Dāvids's eyes. Soon Latvia would be free again. If only Papus could be here to celebrate with them.

They passed the bombed-out farm and in moments their own place came into view. The winter rye would be ready for harvest soon. Beyond it were the newly seeded fields of barley. The rows of tiny new plants gave a delicate green cast to the dark earth. In one pasture Rolfs slowly drove the cows homeward. Stulbenis heard them, and though he barked joyously, he didn't desert his post.

Dāvids looked at the farm with pride. There was the big white two-story house and the huge thatch-roofed dairy barn that housed thirty head of cattle, a stable for ten horses, a cold-storage room, and space to store hay at each end. Then there were the grainery, the chicken house, the pig barn, the blacksmith shop and toolshed, and the wood storage shed, as well as the cabins for the farmhands, the tall windmill, the painted fence lining the long drive out to the road, and the colorful flowers around the house. It was a prosperous farm—with electricity, a telephone, and running water.

With contempt Dāvids thought of the Russians when they first came. The soldiers had been told they were coming to "liberate" Latvia from the crushing bonds of poverty. Yet the Latvian farms made a mockery of their propaganda. The Russians viewed these prosperous farms with envy. They had nothing in their homeland to compare with them. And the Russian-controlled farms were shabby compared with the ones owned by the Latvians. So it became the Russian aim to destroy every successful Latvian farm eventually. They had destroyed some—but Papus had defied them always, keeping his own place in as good repair as possible. It was as though he flaunted before them the lie of their propaganda.

Dāvids wouldn't let himself think of the future—of the harvest to come. With only Rolfs to help, they would never be able to gather enough to carry them through the winter. What they needed were at least two or three good husky men—more would be better. Oskars had not been able to find extra help yet. However, he pitched in whenever he could. As a bookkeeper in a brick factory near Glūda, he had little time to do farming. Yet in the evenings and on weekends he chopped wood, picked fruit, or even churned butter if that needed doing.

Two days later Dāvids and Māmiņa were in the barn trying to finish the milking when Stulbenis raced to the far end of the building where the hay was stored and began barking furiously. Grabbing a pitchfork, Dāvids edged closer to where the dog danced about, yapping shrilly. Then his heart leaped into his throat when he saw the sole of a boot sticking out of the hay!

"Come out—carefully!" he ordered, "or I'll ram you with my pitchfork." Māmiņa came up behind, also carrying a pitchfork.

Slowly a black-haired man shook off the hay and rose to his feet. His face was gaunt and unusually pale, his clothes were bloodstained, and he stood slouched as if it was painful to use one leg.

"Peter Krekov!" Dāvids and Māmiņa exclaimed simultaneously, recognizing the man who had once worked for them. But the dog continued to bark. Not being a protector, only all noise, he didn't attack.

"Shut up!" Dāvids ordered. Then he glared at Peter. "What're you doing here?"

"Hiding," came the answer in the familiar deep voice.

Māmiņa brandished her pitchfork. "We don't want you here."

To Dāvids, Peter was no longer the man who had once worked for them. He represented all the Bolsheviks in Latvia, and his hate for them blazed like a crown fire. "Get out!" he screeched, and with all his pent-up loathing he rushed him with the pitchfork, wanting to hear Peter scream even as the NKVD had made him scream.

One tine caught Peter on the shoulder, and he grunted in surprise as blood spurted from a deep gash and flowed down his already bloody shirt. Then he leaped clumsily away. "I can't get beyond the German lines now—"

"I don't care about your problems," Dāvids growled, but the sight of the ugly wound he himself had just inflicted held him from charging again. "Just get off our place."

With a sigh, Peter turned to walk out, and his knees buckled so that he crumbled into the hay.

"Oh dear, he's sick—and hurt," Māmiņa said in dismay. "We can't kick him out yet, Dāvid. He needs food."

"But Māmin—he's a Russian—our enemy!" Dāvids exclaimed in outrage.

"I'm aware of that. But we are Latvians—and Christians," came Māmiņa's retort. "Can you walk at all?" she asked Peter and he nodded. "Dāvid, help him to the cabin." Without waiting for a reply, she spoke again to Peter. "We'll bring you some food. And I'll come clean that wound."

"Thank you," Peter murmured.

"You needn't thank me," Māmiņa said testily. "As soon as you're taken care of, you'll have to leave."

Still clutching his pitchfork and fighting to control the rage within himself, Dāvids helped Peter to his feet. He was shocked at how old Peter looked. He knew he was only twenty-eight, yet he looked fifty! The man stumbled along, favoring his injured left leg, as he leaned heavily on Dāvids's shoulder. He was near collapse when they reached the cabin.

An hour later Māmiņa had cleaned a bullet hole in his hip, a deep gash on one shoulder, and the pitchfork wound on the other. His left ankle was also swollen and sprained. After hungrily eating a bowl of soup and rye bread, Peter fell asleep.

By the next morning Peter was delirious with fever, and Dāvids and Kārlis were forced against their wishes to alternately sit at his bedside to bathe his body with cool water.

"I think he's a spy," Kārlis's said one time. "I bet he kills us."

Knowing Kārlis's wild imagination and timid nature, Dāvids ignored the comment. He didn't care what Peter was. He was Russian, and that was enough. He had to go.

Every night since the beating, Dāvids had had night-mares that left him trembling and in cold sweats. Always they were the same. He would see the black hose coming at him, and he would hear the question, "Do you have a radio?" It was strange, a lot of what Comrade Shimkevich had asked him, he couldn't remember. But that one question always stood out—probably because it was the only one he could recall admitting to them. In his dreams he would see himself nodding, then a steam shovel would reach down and snatch Papus up in its steel claws. All Dāvids could see of him was his arms and legs as he thrashed around, trying to get free. He would hear screaming, but it didn't seem to come from Papus. It was like it was coming from deep inside Dāvids himself. Sometimes in that picture he would see the Latvian flag, and he would hear the anthem—like he knew Papus was fighting for his country. The dream always ended the same—with Papus, all torn and bloody—being dumped on a mountainous pile of other bodies, one arm flung out, its finger pointing straight at Dāvids. He would waken with a crushing sense of guilt, sobbing into his pillow so as not to waken his brother.

For three days following Peter's arrival, the nightmares showed Peter sitting at the desk instead of Comrade Shimkevich. Each morning, when Dāvids was forced to take food to him, or to help Māmiņa change the dressings, it seemed almost more than he could bear to look at the man and not want to kill him. When he watched Māmiņa cleaning the inflamed wounds, he wanted to yell at her, "Hurt him! Hurt him! Make him scream! Let him die!" And he had to constantly remind himself that it had not been Peter Krekov at that desk.

But Peter was Russian—and that made him guilty, too.

So intense was the battle going on inside Dāvids that he ate little and spoke even less. Kārlis, who usually pestered him and tagged around constantly, found it simpler to avoid his brother.

On the third morning, waking out of a nightmare, Dāvids rose and dressed himself—feeling the need to get out of the house—to do something. As he walked out the back door, the first rays of the rising sun touched the tree in the backyard and he breathed deeply, trying to wash the conflict out of his mind. A sense of peace came over him at the thought that from now on he would do like Papus always had done—be the first one up. No matter how many hired hands Papus had, he'd always prided himself on being an early riser—as hard a worker as any man on his place. Now Dāvids would do the same.

He strode purposefully to the barn. He would feed the cows and hogs. Then he paused at the barn door—confused and angry. Peter was just finishing the job.

"What're *you* doing here?" he demanded, resentment crowding out all other thoughts. How dare Peter do this to him?

"Trying to pay back a little kindness shown me," came the quiet reply.

It was on Dāvids's tongue to tell him to get out—to get off the farm. But they were so far behind in their work, being shorthanded. He decided he would get some use out of this Bolshevik for a few days. The very thought of Peter being here rankled, but the need for help was great.

With a shrug of disdain he walked off and busied himself at other tasks. But his momentary sense of peace was gone, and at breakfast he ate almost nothing, while

Māmiņa clucked worriedly about him, threatening to send him to the doctor to see if he had actually been hurt internally.

Peter did nothing strenuous, but by the end of the day he'd done considerable work, though he looked exhausted. The next day he did more, and by the third day he was chopping wood and patching the pigsty fence.

That night, after Peter left the dinner table to hobble back to his cabin, and Rolfs and the cook, Marta, had gone to their rooms, Māmiņa slowly put her teacup down. "I think he's well enough now," she said, bitterness making her mouth tight. "Tomorrow he has to go."

"I'll bet he's a spy!" This from Kārlis, who squirmed uneasily in his seat. "I bet he'll kill us before he leaves."

"Oh shut up, Kārli," Dāvids said irritably. He had something important to say to Māmiņa, and he didn't need that silly kind of talk. He sat doodling on the tablecloth with his fork, his insides knotting at the reaction he knew he would get when he made his suggestion. But he was determined to have his way.

"I think we should keep Peter," he said.

"No! He's a spy!" Kārlis cried out, his round face going pale. "Send him away."

"Dāvid, you can't be serious!" Māmiņa exclaimed. "He's—he's a Bolshevik!"

"And a darned good farmhand." Dāvids put his fork down and leaned forward on his elbows. All day long he had battled with himself, his hate for Peter conflicting with his need for farm help. But he wanted to keep this farm going as Papus had done. "Māmin, Peter worked here before. Papus said he was the best helper we ever had—"

"Maybe so, but you notice he got rid of him as soon as he could—"

"Do you know that for sure?"

Māmiņa scowled. "What do you mean?"

"Or did Peter leave on his own? He strikes me as a guy who does pretty much what he wants to do."

"All the more reason to get rid of him," Kārlis cut in.

"He—he scares me—he's so—so—big—so *Russian*," Māmiņa said and nervously stirred her tea.

Dāvids understood her feelings. To the short, slender Ozolses, Peter's size was imposing. And his taciturn manner was unnerving. But he was a worker, and right now that's all that mattered.

"Māmin, do you think we can run this farm—you, me, a seven-year-old boy, a woman who has never worked outside on a farm, and a sickly old man?"

"Oskars will find us some help."

"And until then?"

"Oh, I don't care what happens," she said irritably, tears coming to her eyes. "With Jānis gone, I really don't care. I'd rather get a house in Jelgava and go to work to—"

"Leave the farm!" Dāvids was stunned. His square jaw got a set look, and the hazel eyes flashed with indignation. "Papus loved this farm—and I'm not about to give it up."

Māmiņa was white around the mouth. "Dāvid—the Bolsheviks killed your father—or deported him to a living hell," she said with fury. "Have you forgotten? Could you look at that man out there and not remember that?"

"I think of it every time I look at him. And I remember what they did to me." Dāvids rose and began pacing. "Māmin—I won't give up this farm. I won't. Oskars says I'm not a child anymore. Well, one of the signs of maturity is the ability to think of priorities, not prejudices."

Earlier today his thoughts had gone back two years,

when Papus had almost lost the farm because a Jewish banker foreclosed on their mortgage so a friend could buy up this choice piece of land. It was a sudden loan from Oskars that kept Papus from losing it. True, such behavior was rare among the Jewish businessmen they knew. Yet Papus had eventually risked much to help a Jewish man. The priority—to help an innocent man escape death—had overridden Papus's fresh prejudice. To keep the farm Dāvids needed Peter. "The farm is my priority," he said firmly.

Māmiņa looked up at the set jaw, the straight mouth, the eyes that defied her, and she sighed. "Oh, Dāvid, you're so much like your father—so determined—so sure you're right." She shrugged, as though dismissing all responsibility. "As far as I'm concerned, the farm is yours. Without Jānis, it means nothing to me. Do what you want."

Dāvids looked at his mother, unable to comprehend such an attitude. Papus had worked hard, despite the Russian interference, to make this farm a success. Now Māmiņa wanted to leave, to give it up. Every fiber of his being wanted to fight—to defy the tyranny that threatened them.

Māmiņa's words, however, wiped away a little of his self-deprecation. The farm was his—at least as far as Māmiņa was concerned. By hanging onto it, making it succeed, he could in some small way atone for betraying Papus.

In the morning, when Māmiņa told Peter that he could remain and work on the farm, he merely nodded, and as soon as breakfast was over, he went out to the barn. Not to be outdone, Dāvids worked alongside him for hours and Peter didn't say more than a dozen words. But then he had never been much of a talker—not even when Papus had been here.

That night, in utter exhaustion, Dāvids slept without nightmares. He woke at dawn and hurried through the rain to the barn, determined to get there ahead of Peter. But Peter was moving hay so a leak in the roof didn't drip on it.

"Who told you to move that hay?" Dāvids demanded. Under the hay were a few of the cases of vodka he and Oskars had gotten and had not yet buried in pits.

"It'll mould in here if it stays wet."

"Then let it mould."

Peter eyed him warily, as though debating whether or not to argue. Then he nodded his head toward the hay. "Why not move it *and* the vodka?" he suggested. "That way everything stays dry."

Dāvids stiffened, eyeing him suspiciously.

"Well, do we move it?" Peter asked after a while.

Dāvids hated him because he was Russian, but he hated him even more because he knew they had stuff hidden under the hay and he was baiting him.

"Move it," he muttered, and took his frustrations out in hard work—lifting the hay and the cases of vodka. He kept watching Peter. God, how he worked! For a man who had been so pale and sick, he sure had recovered. Dāvids couldn't help wonder how much else he knew about them, and this made him nervous. He wondered if he'd done the right thing—keeping Peter.

CHAPTER 6

ALL WEEK Oskars did not come to the farm, though he talked to Māmiņa often on the telephone. Nor had the family seen much of Daila. Finally on Sunday she came for a visit, looking thin and worried. She had heard nothing from Valdis since he'd gone into hiding the night Papus was taken away—over three weeks before. As usual, Oskars arrived in time for dinner.

In sharp contrast to his normal restraint, today Oskars was bursting with news, and he began talking the moment he shook hands all around and then sat down at the table. Jelgava was a beehive of activity. "Soldiers everywhere—tanks—guns—you never saw such artillery. And planes! I hear they're pushing on—clear to Moscow—they'll drive those Russian snakes all the way across their own land. Oh, I tell you—that German army is something to see. Makes the Bolsheviks look like clods. Do you know, they're already repairing the bombed-out airport. And at the brick factory we're working overtime. That's why I haven't been out."

"I hear on the radio that we're already setting up our own civil government in Riga," Māmiņa said, scowling as she carved a slice of ham. "But I'm also hearing that things aren't quite the way we want them."

Oskars's face clouded as he thoughtfully buttered a slice of dark rye bread. "In a way you're right. The Germans have taken over all the major business—"

"Just like the Bolsheviks," Dāvids said in despair. "They go back and forth across Latvia like we're a highway open to them and not to us."

"Well, not exactly," Oskars argued. "These Germans aren't beasts like the Bolsheviks. At least they're human. Toward us, that is." He shook his head sadly. "But the poor Jews—"

Dāvids cringed. Poor old Jēkabs. What would become of him?

As though to change the gloomy talk, Oskars turned to Daila and grinned, giving her a wink. "Guess who I saw today."

Instant hope flared on her pretty face, and quickly she put down the milk pitcher. "Valdis? Oh, Oskar, don't tease me—was it Valdis?" Then she frowned. "In Jelgava?" Oskars nodded. "What was he doing?" she asked breathlessly, grabbing his hand in both of hers. "Oh, tell me!"

Oskars kissed her hands. "He was keeping law and order, my love," he said gently.

"They—the Nazis, I mean—they *know* he's a Latvian soldier?"

"Valdis is a soldier?" Kārlis asked in wide-eyed astonishment.

Oskars nodded. "He sure is, young fellow—and a fine one. Like so many of the Latvian army, he decided to come out of hiding. The Nazis said they wanted the Latvians to help them establish proper rule here."

Daila beamed, clasping her hands in front of herself in sheer ecstacy. "Oh, I'm so proud of him!"

"Bah!" Māmiņa said and set the teapot down hard. "We changed one tyrant for another—Stalin for Hitler—NKVD for Gestapo. I don't trust either one of them—never have! Valdis is a fool to expose himself—"

"Now, Māmin," Daila said soothingly, "he knows what he's doing."

Māmiņa gave a grunt of disbelief and the talk went on about other things. Finally the table was cleared and the dishes washed, and everyone went out into the backyard. Oskars threw balls at Kārlis and Dāvids.

Suddenly Peter Krekov walked out of the barn, and without looking toward the family, he headed away to the cabin.

"Good God—what's *he* doing here?" Oskars demanded in disbelief.

"He's working here," Dāvids spoke up. He watched Māmiņa walk to the back step and sit down beside Daila, tucking her skirt under her. He had wondered if she had told Oskars, but evidently she'd been afraid to. Even now, she was saying nothing, letting her son face an angry man peering indignantly through his glasses.

"Are you crazy, Elita?" Oskars roared. "That—that *scum*—"

"Oskar," Dāvids spoke up, trying to remain calm, "we can't run this farm with just Rolfs. We aren't thrilled about having a Russian here. But we can't be choosy right now. Peter knows farming and he's—"

"Nonsense. There are many Latvians you can get who know farming. Besides, what's he doing in Latvia at all? He should be back in Rus—"

"He'd been hurt. We found him hiding here. If Papus was here, I'm sure he would've—"

"*If* your Papus was here!" Oskars's face was livid. "It's because of that kind of snake that he *isn't* here." He turned to Māmina. "Elita, you must get rid of him—immediately. He could be—"

"No!" Dāvids cut in, his legs spraddled in a defiant stance and his jaw set. "This is my farm. I say he stays. I need his help—"

Oskars stared, unbelieving. "*Your* farm?" he asked in blank surprise. Then he turned to Māmiņa. "Elita, what is this kid babbling about?"

Māmiņa shook her head slowly as she sighed. "You said he was grown up. All right—let him run the place. I can't."

Oskars was speechless as he stared first at Māmiņa, then Daila and Kārlis sitting silently watching the argument. Then he glared at Peter disappearing into his cabin. "A Bolshevik on Jānis's farm. And Jānis dead because of Bolsheviks! It's wrong, I tell you—it's—it's immoral—it's disgraceful!" He turned his angry glance back to Dāvids and shook his head. "You disappoint me, Dāvid."

"I'm sorry," Dāvids replied sadly. "But it seems right to me."

A few days later Daila called, bubbling with joy, to say that Valdis was now coming home each night. The Police Battalion, which consisted of the soldiers who had been in hiding and who had been supplied with smuggled guns, were now being absorbed into the German army, and they would be put to work policing and maintaining order in Latvia. She sounded so proud to think that her husband was a soldier defending his country.

In the meantime, Peter Krekov proved to be a godsend

for the Ozols family, patching the leaking barn roof, cleaning the grainery, rebuilding the hogpen, and repairing the broken fence. Except for coming into the kitchen to eat, he never set foot in the house and he kept to himself. Having worked here before, Peter had no need of orders. He knew what had to be done.

Though Oskars made it clear that he disapproved of Peter working on the farm, he was forced to admit that his dislike of Peter was based solely on the fact that the man was a Russian. He knew nothing about him and had scarcely ever spoken to him even when he had been here before.

Because Oskars could come out only on Sundays these days because of the press of overtime work, and Peter was never up at the house on Sundays, Peter had been working for several months and the men had not yet come face to face.

Then one Thursday evening, while Māmiņa, Dāvids, Kārlis, Peter, Rolfs, and Marta were all eating dinner, Oskars bicycled out from Glūda. His arm was healed, and the haggard look was gone from his thin face. Evidently hard work and long hours had pushed the tragedy back in his mind so that he could think of other things now. Only the sad, haunted look behind the steel-rimmed glasses told that he still remembered.

"Come in, Oskar, dear," Māmiņa said when he appeared at the back door. Oskars entered and immediately went around the table shaking hands. Peter, sitting across from Dāvids, stiffened, then put down his fork. When Oskars got around to him, Peter hesitated, looking like he would not shake hands. At the last moment he extended his big callused hand and briefly touched Oskars'. He said nothing, but merely nodded coldly. Watching Peter obliquely, Dāvids saw him casually drop his hand to his lap, as though to wipe it on his pants before picking up his fork again.

Oskars sat down and poured himself a cup of tea. "I came to see if you have a jar of honey you could spare." At Māmiņa's puzzled look, he explained. "Daila called me—in tears. Valdis is to be sent to eastern Latvia—near the border. Well, it seems that my Nazi boss is unhappy because sugar is hard to get here, and he likes sweetening in his coffee." Oskars gave his shy smile. "I sort of implied I might know where I could find some honey. He asked me what he could do to get some, and I explained about Valdis. He said the captain in charge of the Police Battalion was his friend, and he'd fix it so Valdis would stay in Jelgava."

"Oh, Oskar, you're a dear!" Māmiņa exclaimed.

"Thank you for the dinner," Peter said coldly, wiping his mouth on his napkin. He rose. "I have much to do." Stiffly he walked out.

A momentary silence fell over the room, as though Peter's departure signified disapproval. Then Māmiņa turned to Davids. "Go out to the cold-storage room, dear, and get a jar of honey."

Curious about Peter's abrupt departure, Dāvids was only too happy to leave the house. Before getting the honey, he watched Peter walk over and stand by the windmill, staring off across the fields. The set of the broad shoulders and the spraddle-legged stance denoted anger—aggression. To Dāvids he embodied in his pose everything Russian. Dāvids couldn't see his eyes, but he was sure he would have seen hate in them. He tried to think back to when Peter had been here before, but he couldn't remember any particular animosity at that time.

Peter had been a hired hand, Oskars a friend of the owner, and each man had shown the proper deference to the other.

He got a jar of honey, noticing that there were only five large jars left. The beehives, over in the woods where the Russians had not known about them, would yield more honey soon. Since none of this was included in the quotas demanded by the occupation government, it was used by the family primarily in black-market sales. A liter of honey these days brought high prices because of the sugar shortage.

During the next few days Dāvids tried subtle ways of questioning Peter about Oskars, but Peter ignored all attempts. Finally one day they were out plowing and Peter paused to wipe his sweating face. In this distance they could see Oskars bicycling toward the house.

Dāvids's curiosity became too great to resist, and he decided on the direct questioning method. "Peter, do you know Oskars Mitulis? I mean, have you had dealings with him?"

"No." Peter kicked mud off his boots, using a stick to pry loose a clod under his heel.

"How come you hate him then—didn't want to shake hands with him?"

Peter threw him a wary glance, as though surprised that Dāvids had noticed. Then he turned back to his plowing. "I don't like that kind of man," he said and immediately walked away. Dāvids knew Peter would answer no more questions.

As he watched Peter, he could understand a little how a big, broad-shouldered, physically virile young man like Peter would have only contempt for a thin, slump-shouldered, pinch-faced little bookkeeper who had held the same job in the same factory for over twenty years, meekly obeying his Latvian employers, then his Russian ones, and now his Nazi one—conniving with them for special favors. Though Dāvids understood Peter's feelings, his loyalty to the lifelong family friend and his godfather made him resent Peter's attitude.

It was mid-September, and school had started once again when Oskars finally found some farm workers. One was a burly Latvian named Verners who'd lost two fingers during the bombing of Riga's airport and could no longer do skilled manual labor in a bicycle factory. Since he'd been raised on a farm, he adjusted well, and Māmiņa gave him one of the bachelor rooms at the end of the house, where Rolfs and Marta also had rooms. The other man was a wiry little Latvian named Gunārs, and he and his family lost their home when Jelgava's airport was bombed. Gunārs brought his wife, Elza, and his seven-year-old twin boys to the farm, and they lived in the cabin next to Peter.

Oskars tried every way he knew to convince Dāvids to get rid of Peter, now that he had all the extra help, but Dāvids refused, and Māmiņa would not intervene. She ran the house, as she always had, and left the running of the farm to her thirteen-year-old son, even as she had left it to her husband.

"I'll get another man—a Latvian," Oskars persisted, and still Dāvids said no. He would have liked to have had Peter gone, because his presence was a constant reminder of the beating, but deep in his heart he knew he could not run the farm without Peter. He knew too little about it and Peter—having been here before—knew much.

Oskars's disappointment in Dāvids soon gave way to grudging admiration. "By golly, I always said that if you put your mind to something—you'd make it work," he said one morning when Dāvids walked him around the farm, showing the fields deep in grain, the barn in good repair, and the dairy cows producing a record yield of milk. "I hate to admit it, but you were right, insisting on keeping Peter. He's a big help." He put an arm across Dāvids's shoulder. "You're growing up, my boy— assuming responsibilities. Jānis would be proud of you."

Dāvids cringed at the praise. Still vivid in his memory was Papus walking out without looking at his battered son, knowing he had weakened and betrayed him.

One day a Nazi officer came to the house to say that the farm was now the property of the German Third Reich but that the family would be allowed to manage the place in accordance with instructions. Dāvids learned that meant they had high quotas to meet and the prices paid for produce was low.

"We won't be able to survive," Māmiņa complained after the man left.

"Oh, yes, we will," Dāvids replied firmly. Every nerve in him rebelled at the thought of the Nazis owning his land. The Germans had led them to believe they would be free. But the German was no better than the Soviet. Dāvids remembered Oskars telling him, "Don't you forget—your father fought to make Latvia free." In him was born the desire to resist the new conquerors. He would find some way to free his land. In the meantime he would do as Papus had done—handle black-market goods. He thought of the hidden beehives, of the peat bog that the Russians—and now the Nazis—knew nothing about, of the extra butter, hams, and bacon in the larder. And the Nazi quotas stated that they would be paid partly in marks, and partly in coupons for vodka and cigarettes. Māmiņa exploded. "What do we need with vodka and cigarettes? We don't smoke or drink—not that much." But Dāvids was pleased. The supply of cigarettes in Latvia since the war was always chaotic at best, so they would buy up supplies with their coupons when cigarettes were plentiful, and they would sell them during shortages. This would provide a far better income than if the Nazis paid them outright for the farm produce. As for vodka—it was the best commodity of all and always brought high prices.

A few days later, Dāvids went around the farm and took an inventory of everything they had hidden away. There was far less than he had realized. Papus must have spent a fortune on the wedding! But it only intensified his determination to make the farm succeed—despite the Germans—as Papus had defied all Russian attempts to ruin him.

Dāvids resisted going back to school. For one thing, school under the Nazis was not much different from school under the Russians. Instead of Latvian history, they had learned about Communism—now it was Nazi propaganda. Instead of learning Lettish, they had learned Russian; they now learned German. And Dāvids's fierce pride in his own country rebelled. He tried explaining to Māmiņa that he needed to stay home and supervise the farm—but for once Māmiņa was adamant. He was to go to school. Consequently he was forced to turn over to Peter more of the running of the farm.

Something about Peter intrigued him. That he was an excellent farmer, there was no question; but he was definitely a loner—a man of intense feelings—and a man of mystery. It made Dāvids want to penetrate that armor. But Peter's armor seemed inpenetrable and as the months went by, Dāvids knew no more about him than he had known the day he found him.

In the meantime Latvia's bright hope for freedom faded fast, as the Nazis established their own officials at the head of the government. Conditions were not much different from when the Russians had ruled, except perhaps the Nazis were not quite as brutal.

Or so everyone thought. Then one Sunday afternoon the Ozols family drove to Glūda to visit Daila. Maybe, with luck, Valdis would be home for the day. When Daila greeted them at the door, her face was tearstained and she looked ill. Dāvids's heart leaped to his throat—something must have happened to Valdis!

"Come in," she said in a choked voice. But as soon as Dāvids stepped inside, he saw Valdis standing by a window, his face pale and drawn as he stared out across the fields. The only thing Dāvids could imagine was that his reprieve, paid for by a jar of honey, had ended and he was being sent to the Latvian-Russian border.

"What—what happened?" he asked. Māmiņa, sensing something tragic, put her arm around Daila and stroked her blond hair.

"Jēkabs," Daila murmured. "He's dead."

"Jēkabs? The Jew who owned the country store?" Kārlis asked.

"How did he die?" Māmiņa asked when Daila nodded.

There was a long silence, and the longer it lasted, the tighter Dāvids's chest felt.

"I shot him," Valdis murmured finally, not looking around.

"You!" Dāvids couldn't believe his ears. Valdis had loved Jēkabs as much as the rest of the family. "How could you!"

Valdis spun around, fury burning on his face. "Do you think I *wanted* to, you idiot?!" His jaw muscles worked spasmodically and he hunched his shoulders forward while his fists clenched. "They lined them up—they never had a chance—"

"Who lined what?" Kārlis cut in.

"The Gestapo—rounded up the Jews—lined them in a row by open graves—made Latvian soldiers shoot them." His voice broke on a sob that wrenched his body. "A stinking polecat of a Nazi—held a gun at my head—told me to shoot or I'd die—six of us had to shoot the Jews—about twenty. I saw Jēkabs look at me." He shuddered, remembering.

"He *saw* you kill him?" Dāvids asked in horror.

Valdis seemed almost to strangle on the words as he told the story. "This morning—it happened. Jēkabs knew I couldn't do it—" He looked pleadingly at them all. "I've known him since I was a boy. He used to tell me I was—was like a son to him—" A sob choked off his words momentarily, then he looked up and spoke in an agonizing whisper. "Jēkabs had a son—he told me once that he saw him occasionally—in secret, of course—to protect him." He hung his head. "I couldn't shoot Jēkabs. I couldn't!" His shoulders sagged. "He looked at me—said, 'Go ahead, my boy. I'm old and tired anyway. I can't hide anymore. Daila needs you. Go ahead and shoot. I understand." Tears ran down Valdis's face as he relived the horror. "I closed my eyes—pulled the trigger—when I opened—Jēkabs dead—they pushed him into a grave—" Again his voice choked in this throat. "Oh God, forgive me," he moaned and covered his face. From behind his hands came the agonizing cry, "Poor old Jēkabs." He swung around and looked out the window again. Then he yelled, "Beasts—just like the Bolsheviks!" He gave a nasty, angry laugh. "Liberators! Hah! More like murderers!" He stomped out of the room, slamming the door behind him.

Dāvids's own private misery engulfed him. Once again he saw Jēkabs telling how Papus had hidden him on the farm. "Stupid me," he berated himself silently. "I didn't realize he wanted me to hide him again. I'd heard that the Germans were hard on Jews. And all I'd done was feel sorry for the poor fellow." He remembered how he had resented seeing Jēkabs because it reminded him that Papus might also be a hunted man, hated by his captors. Filled with self-loathing, he realized he was not, and never could be, the man his father had been. Papus had thought of others—he was concerned only with himself. Knowing this made him cringe in shame. He wanted to crawl into some dark corner and hide. Poor scared Jēkabs. He knew after he had spoken that his fate was sealed—sealed by an uncaring thirteen-year-old kid.

What had begun as a sunny Sunday afternoon ride, filled with joy and anticipation, ended in gloom as they turned the wagon homeward. Inwardly Dāvids churned with impatience. The Nazis had to be stopped! But what could he do? He felt so helpless—and frustrated.

When they reached the farm, Verners was doing the evening milking. Only essential chores were done on Sunday—and usually two of the three men alternately had the day off.

"Dāvid, go see if Peter is around," Māmiņa said as she headed to the house. "Tell him I'd like to see him about a leaky faucet."

Dāvids nodded and headed for the barn, but Peter wasn't there. "Verner, have you seen Peter?" he asked as he went over to where Verners was finishing the milking.

"No—haven't seen him all day."

Dāvids went to the small cabin and knocked. But there was no answer. The door was unlocked, and though he knew it was wrong to enter while Peter was away, his curiosity was too strong, and he stepped inside, hoping to

find some clue about this man. The cabin was im-
maculate—and starkly bare.

"Looking for me?" came the deep voice behind him,
and Dāvids spun around, guilt on his face.

"M-Māmiņa wants to talk to you," he stammered,
aware of the pinpoints of fury flashing in Peter's eyes.
Then, as though a shade was pulled down, no emotion in
the dark eyes showed.

"Tell her I'll be up in a minute," Peter stepped
aside—a clear gesture that Dāvids was to leave.

As Dāvids walked out, he noticed with surprise that
Peter's boots were muddy—wet mud. On a farm such a
thing was fairly common, except that for the past week
there had been no rain and the plowed fields were
unusually dry.

Dāvids was sure he had his first clue about this strange
man.

CHAPTER 7

DĀVIDS'S SUDDEN elation that he had a clue about Peter's mysterious wandering soon faded when he realized that there were marshes everywhere. Peter could have easily taken a shortcut from Glūda, or from the town of Auce, or almost anywhere, by cutting across one of the marshes.

He needed to be busy, he realized, to drive out his depressing and suspicious thoughts. So he went to the big grainery building to begin moving all of the hidden items in preparation for tomorrow. As was the custom in Latvia, all the various grain crops of rye, wheat, oats, barley, or whatever that were grown on a farm were put in the *šķūnis*, the immense drying building, after cutting, to await the day of threshing. Then neighbors would gather and one of them would bring a thresher. All day the men worked, threshing the piles of grain. If the crop were large, it might take several days to get the job done. Then the neighbors would all go to the next farm, and the next, until everyone's crop was threshed. In Latvia such a thing was known as *talka* — neighbors helping neighbors.

Since the threshing crew would arrive in the morning and there would be many people moving the grain, it was imperative that Dāvids hide the black-market goods elsewhere for a while.

He put all the cartons of cigarettes into a gunnysack and carried them to the woodshed. They had cashed in their first coupons, and adding what he had gotten the day he and Oskars went out, he now had seventeen cartons. "Money in the bank," he chortled. But when he finally came to the supply of vodka, he was no longer laughing. There should have been eleven cases. There were only eight!

He slumped down on a bag of grain—totally bereft. Papus was dead, Jēkabs was dead, the Nazis had not given them their freedom, Valdis was in despair, Oskars was a broken man, they had a Bolshevik on the farm, Māmiņa was withdrawing into herself and wasn't interested in the farm, the nightmares were eating away at his own soul—and now this! Someone was stealing their supplies. He knew Māmiņa had not taken any, because she always told him when she did so he could alter his inventory.

He was head of the family now—he was a man—and a man couldn't cry. Angrily he brushed away tears. "Oh Papu," he murmured, "why aren't you here?" He felt overwhelmed by all his troubles. He wasn't ready to grow up and be a man.

Suddenly he became aware that he wasn't alone, and when he looked up, Peter stood at the doorway, watching him. The mud on his boots was gone.

Because there were still traces of tears on Dāvids's face, he searched his mind for a quick, acceptable explanation as to why a man would cry. He couldn't admit defeat —not to Peter of all people.

"My friend was killed this morning," he said. Typical of Peter, he made no comment. "He was a Jew—Jēkabs was his name—the Nazis made Valdis kill him this morning." The need to pour out some of his inner misery, caused in part by the horror of this morning, made the words tumble out. "They made the Jews kneel by a grave. Peter—Jēkabs never did a mean thing in his life! He was just a quiet, kind man who sold farm supplies and gave candy to kids. He was just a harmless Jew—and now he's dead."

There was a long silence as Dāvids sat slumped in his own anguish, staring at the floor. Finally Peter spoke in a flat voice. "War is hell, Dāvid. But we can't cry for the dead. It's the ones who are still alive that matter." Dāvids looked up, puzzled, but there was no expression on Peter's face. It was almost like a mask, he thought peevishly.

"Well, I must get to the house. Your mother is waiting," Peter said, his voice still flat and empty, and he turned and walked away.

Dāvids stared after him. How like a Bolshevik —cold—without feelings. The Russians hated capitalists, and most of the Jews were well-to-do. So probably Peter was pleased to learn that more Jews were dying.

Oppressed by his tangled emotions, Dāvids stood up and squared his shoulders. As Peter said, it was the living that mattered. And tomorrow would be a busy day. He wouldn't be going to school because all hands were needed, and he looked forward to a day of strenuous work. In the meantime, he moved the remaining eight cases of vodka.

Shortly after dawn the next morning, men arrived from neighboring farms—men Dāvids had known all his life—and the work of threshing began. The men remembered Peter from his previous time on the farm, and they accepted him, knowing his abilities. Dāvids worked as hard as any of them, lifting the grain with a pitchfork and feeding it into the thresher. They paused only when Māmiņa brought lunch for everyone. Soon the air was thick again with the dust of flying chaff, and the distant chickens clucked disapprovingly at the clanking noise.

It was close to five in the afternoon, near stopping time because of fall's earlier twilight, when Dāvids saw Kārlis galloping home on Berta, the old gray horse. Normally the boys did not ride horses to school, but Kārlis had not wanted to walk home alone, knowing that if he were to walk, it would be dark before he reached the farm. So Māmiņa had said he could use Berta.

Dāvids scowled as he watched his brother. They were forbidden to gallop Berta because she was unpredictable. But Kārlis, not having his older brother along to dissuade him, and driven by his fear of the dark, was whipping Berta with a birch switch, urging her along. He turned into the lane, and suddenly Berta heard the clanking of the thresher. Unused to this ungainly, noisy machine on her home farm, she shied in wild-eyed terror, leaped over the white fence, and bolted across the field. With arms and legs splaying out, Kārlis sailed out of the saddle, hit the fence, and tumbled in a heap to the ground.

"Kārli!" Dāvids screamed and tossed down his pitch-fork, racing the long distance to his brother. Kārlis didn't move.

Dāvids was breathing hard when he reached him, and he gently turned the boy over. An ugly lump on his forehead distorted the cherubic face, and blood stained the fair hair. But it was the leg that made Dāvids wince in sympathy. It was badly broken below the knee, so that his foot stuck out at an odd angle. Māmiņa, Peter, and

Gunārs came running up, and Māmiņa knelt beside him, cradling his head in her lap as she cried.

"I'll get a wagon," Peter said and went back to the buildings while Gunārs headed across the field after Berta. In a short while Peter returned and gently lifted Kārlis onto a blanket he'd laid in the wagon bed. "He should be taken to the hospital," he said.

"The nearest one is in Jelgava," Māmiņa wailed.

"Then that's where we'll go," Dāvids said, climbing up on the driver's seat. Peter returned to the threshing.

Hours later Kārlis lay in the hospital bed with a bandage around his head and his leg in a cast, looking small and forlorn. The doctor said the head injury was not serious, but the break would necessitate many weeks in a cast, and he wanted Kārlis to remain in the hospital for several days for observation.

"See what happened," Māmiņa said accusingly as she stood looking out the hospital window. "I told you we should have moved into the city. Kārlis wouldn't have gotten hurt."

"Oh Māmiņ," Dāvids said wearily, "he could get hurt tripping over a curb in the city just as easily." He pointed down to two Nazi soldiers using flashlights, who had stopped someone in the street and demanded that he show his identity card. "Besides, in the city you run up against Nazis all the time. At least on the farm they aren't in our hair as much."

Māmiņa sighed. "I guess you're right. Anyway, I'm going to stay here with Kārlis till he can come home. I don't want to leave him here all alone. He's so little."

"Good idea, Māmiņ," Dāvids said and patted her shoulder. "And don't you worry—Kārlis isn't hurt bad. He'll be fine."

He kissed Māmiņa and went down to his wagon. As he

headed out of town, he passed the shadowy form of the big stone building that had housed the NKVD. He shivered as the horror of that night inside there came vividly to him.

A kilometer or two farther he passed an enclosed area. Along the top of the chain link fence were rolls of barbed wire. When passing it while coming to the hospital, Māmiņa had said this was the Jewish ghetto. Here the Nazis kept all Jews until such time as they raided the area and hauled some off to slave labor in Germany, or killed them. They seemed to delight in keeping the Jews here, taking a few at a time so that the others lived in a constant state of terror.

He was just past when a Nazi stepped out of the blackness, a flashlight in his hand. "What're you doing out of the compound?" he demanded.

"I'm not a Jew," Dāvids said, fear tightening his throat. He blinked as the bright beam blinded him to the man.

"Let's see your identification." The voice was ugly, and Dāvids bridled. But obediently he pulled out his card that the Nazis had issued to every Latvian.

"You live south of Glūda, according to this," the soldier said coldly. "What're you doing here?" He jerked his head toward the fenced compound.

"I just took my brother to the hospital—he broke his leg. Now I'm going home. This is the way we came into town, and it's the only way I know how to get out."

The soldier inspected his wagon and even went over the horse carefully as though searching for some hidden contraband. "What hospital?" he demanded and Dāvids named it. "Your brother's name?" Again Dāvids replied. "I'll check," came the retort, and the soldier walked to a guard post that Dāvids had not noticed before. By the light of his big flashlight, the man telephoned. Dāvids sat rigid—afraid because he could so easily be hauled off to headquarters and questioned by the Gestapo, but also seething at the attitude of this hard-faced, accusing Nazi. What right did this German have to invade his nation, then treat him like he was a criminal? He had the same urge to spit on him as he'd spit at the Bolshevik. But he let no expression register on his face.

"Get on home—and don't go riding around at night," the soldier snapped as he stepped out of the guardhouse. The flashlight beam shone directly into Dāvids's face. "Next time you might not get off so easy."

Dāvids nodded stiffly and flipped the reins. He could see little in the dark, but he wasn't concerned. In harness was Melnis—the reliable black horse that he had purchased himself over a year ago. Melnis knew his way instinctively.

As he neared Glūda, he decided it would be safer if he spent the night with Daila and Valdis, and travel home by daylight the next day. Once inside, he telephoned Marta and reported that Kārlis was resting easily and saying he'd be there in the morning.

While he ate, he stared off into space, preoccupied with the memory of the encounter with the Nazi guard.

"You look like you could bite that plate," Daila teased.

"I'd rather bite the Nazis," came the resentful retort. Then his anger exploded. "They have no right here! They're no better than the Bolsheviks—and I'd like to kick them out. I'd like to beat them to a pulp—spit on them—kill them! If there was a way I could get them—"

"Hush, Dāvid," Daila warned. "You could be killed for such—"

"No, let him speak his mind," Valdis cut in. He leaned forward across the table. "Would you *really* like to do something—"

"No, Valdi!" Daila cried out. "No! He's just a boy!"

Dāvids threw his sister a look of annoyance, then focused on his brother-in-law. "What've you got in mind?"

"That depends," Valdis hedged. "A lot of lives hinge on whether others can keep their mouths shut. I think you could be a great help. You didn't break under NKVD torture, and that shows you've got what we need. I wouldn't be saying this, except I think you've proven yourself." Inwardly Dāvids cringed, remembering that somehow he *had* broken. But he knew there was no torture that could ever break him again.

"This would be one way you could pay back what was done to you," he heard Valdis saying, and he grabbed eagerly at the chance. Only by actively doing something could he ever live with himself.

"I can keep my mouth shut," he said, and he was determined that he would.

Daila stated to protest, and Valdis gently covered her hand. "We need him, my love," he said softly. "I wouldn't ask him if I wasn't desperate. And he would be the last kind of person the Nazis would ever suspect." Then to Dāvids he continued. "We have a lot of soldiers who weren't taken in by this Nazi talk of helping to free us." The haunted look came to his eyes as he remembered what he'd been forced to do because he had surfaced as a Latvian soldier. "These men are staying underground. They've even smuggled people out of the country. But they need arms—"

"Guns! I don't even have a pistol!" Dāvids exclaimed.

"Keep your voice down," Valdis reminded him. Then he added in a low voice. "You don't need a pistol. What we need is a go-between. We had someone—but he's gone. He had a hiding place—but only he and the head of the underground knew where it was—"

"Can't that man—?"

"He was killed outright." Dāvids's heart skipped a beat. Valdis's message was all too clear. A go-between lived in danger.

"We need someone the Nazis would never suspect," Valdis continued. "But first of all, we need a place to hide the guns being smuggled to us. When the underground hides the guns, we'll be notified. Then we'll need someone to go get them and deliver them—"

"I'll do it," Dāvids exclaimed eagerly. At last he would be able to actively defend his country. He sat up straighter.

"Dāvid, dear," Daila warned, "if you were caught, it could mean death. You don't—"

"How long have *you* known about all this underground stuff?" he asked her in surprise.

"I knew Valdis was an underground soldier—just like Papus knew. But that's *all* I knew." She looked with pride at her husband. "Until lately—when Valdis said he was going to continue working with the underground. And they need guns. But as an acclaimed soldier, there isn't too much he can do. Also, it looks like he'll be sent away eventually to the border—and he needs someone here—"

"Me," Dāvids said proudly.

She sighed. "I know how you feel. After what happened to you—then Papus—then Jēkabs," she bowed her head. "I wish it didn't have to be you, honey."

Dāvids felt a surge of love for her. She was involved in this battle of freedom, and knowing that he would be, too, made him feel closer to her. "Are you active in it?"

"Sort of. I mean, I know some things, and who some of the soldiers are. But you won't be involved in that way. All you'll have to do is be a go-between. But first we have to find a place to hide the guns—"

"Like we hide the vodka and stuff—in the grainery?"

"Oh Lord, no!" Valdis was horrified. "That would be too risky—with that Bolshevik on the place. Are you crazy?"

"Then where?"

"That's what I don't know yet. But we'll figure something out. It should be out by the farm someplace—maybe the woods."

"We also need some money right now," Daila explained. "Not a great deal—but we've got a few people making false passports, false identification papers, and so forth, and we need ready cash."

Dāvids thought of the few marks in the leather pouch in the attic. But he knew he needed more than that. And he didn't have much vodka left.

"We'll find a way," he said firmly. "There's an answer somewhere."

"Remember," Valdis warned him. "You've got to move *very, very* carefully. The slightest suspicion—"

"I will."

Dāvids slept little that night, thinking of what he'd learned. He knew he was placing himself in danger, but the satisfaction he felt in helping to rid his country of the enemy drove out all fear of reprisal.

He was up at dawn and left before Valdis and Daila had breakfast. Once at home, and while eating, he thought suddenly of the peat bog. Peat was always in demand for fuel, and a wagonload of it, plus what he had in the pouch, would amount to quite a bit of money.

"I won't be able to help with the threshing today," he told Peter. "I'm going to cut peat—we've got expenses to meet."

Peter paused in his eating. "I'll be glad to cut it when we're finished threshing," he said.

"No, you'll have to help the others—*talka*, you know. It's expected."

"We should finish up here by three or four today," Peter persisted. "I could cut in an hour what would take you half a day to do."

Dāvids's jaw got a set look. Though it was true, a man Peter's size could far outwork someone as short and slight as he was, yet he resented Peter saying so. "I'll do it," he said firmly. He could see Peter hesitate as though debating whether to argue, then with a shrug he resumed eating.

After hitching Melnis to the wagon, Dāvids set out toward the back part of the farm, just beyond the dense wall of trees that hid the peat bog. He rode through the deep shade of the forest and thought of the times Papus had ridden through here to cut peat. When he was younger, he'd gone with his father many times. But during the past year Papus had gone alone. Of course, he, Dāvids, had been in school most of that time.

The fall colors added a brightness to the forest, and he rode along feeling more of a sense of peace than he'd felt in a long time. Kārlis's injury had worried him—one more problem added to the many they already had—but this morning he felt confident that they could ride this wave of trouble, too.

He came out of the shade and halted the wagon on the rise of ground and looked out over the bog below. When Papus had first farmed this land, he had drained this bog, and now the peat moss was relatively dry and could be taken out in half-meter slabs to be sold. It was a bleak scene—this bog—with a few trees, but mostly just an endless expanse of dried moss, some heather and grasses, and little else. The peat bog itself was a checker-board—light where no peat had been cut, dark in the worked places. It was like being in another world. People never came over here.

There were now two roads down to the bog—the old one at the far end, where most of the peat had been cut, and the new one here where he was. Though it was clear this new road was the only one being used now, still it was unfamiliar to him, so he drove to the old one and headed down. The old trail was quite overgrown—nobody had been to the bottom in quite a while.

He started down the hill, then stopped—staring in surprise. Not ten meters from the path was a big hole in the ground. Not a hole exactly—more like a cave dug in the side of the hill. From over by the new road it was not visible.

He got down and peered into it. It was deep but clean. Something caught his attention and he crawled into the cave. Picking up a small object, he turned it over, then such a pang of remorse hit him that he sat down, buried his head on his knees, and wished he was dead. He was holding a brass button—like the one missing off Jēkabs's threadbare coat. This was where Papus had hidden their Jewish friend, and Dāvids realized with a pang of guilt that he could just as easily have hidden him here, too. Jēkabs would have shown him where it was, if he had only shown a little compassion. He could picture the hunched, emaciated man sitting here, looking out over the bleak bog, wondering what would become of him. How lonely he must have been, how deserted! He had probably wandered around the bog whenever the weather had been reasonably dry, and used the cave to sleep in and for shelter from the incessant rains. But how miserable and cold it must have been during the time of snows. Dāvids groaned—Jēkabs had helped many, and he had been well loved. But he was a Jew. And for that he had died.

Because he couldn't tolerate his own feelings of guilt, he crawled out and went back to the new road and down into the bog. Picking up the long, flat-bladed shovel, he got to work cutting peat. Then it hit him—the perfect place to hide guns! It was remote—no one would ever know about it. He tackled the job of peat cutting with vigor—excited that in one swoop he'd solved both the money and the hiding-place problems.

By the time he got back, the threshing was finished, all the men and the machine were gone, and Peter was in the barn at the faucet, running the water over his head.

"How'd it go?" he asked, coming up sputtering.

"Fine."

"No problems?"

"Nope."

"You're quite a worker, Dāvid," he said, nodding toward the wagon. "That's a man-sized load you got."

"Almost as much as you would have gotten." Dāvids couldn't resist getting in a dig at Peter. Then he dunked his own sweating head under the cool water.

"You seem disturbed," Peter continued, his voice muffled by the towel as he dried his face.

It was a harmless enough question, but it aroused immediate suspicion in Dāvids as he lifted his head and took the towel from Peter. Peter wasn't one to ask questions, not even the innocent one's like "how'd it go?" or "no problems?". Usually he spoke only to discuss some farm problem.

Peter was waiting for a reply, so he shrugged casually. "Nothing wrong—just bone tired."

As he walked into the kitchen, his mouth watered at the delicious smell of freshly baked rye bread and roasting pork, and Marta bustled around, getting everything on the table.

"You know better than to come in here with muddy boots," she yelled at him when he entered. "Get back outside, young man!"

Dāvids went out and kicked off his boots, and as he did so, he had a mental picture of Peter—his boots caked with mud the other day.

Could he have been at the bog that day? He remembered Peter's insistent offer to go himself, today, instead. Why? He thought of the three missing cases of vodka—but there had been no vodka hidden in the cave. So obviously that wasn't why Peter didn't want him there. His mind searched for reasons, but there was no answer to his questions.

CHAPTER 8

As SOON AS the threshing was done, Dāvids reported to Daila and Valdis that he had found the perfect hiding place.

"It couldn't be better!" Valdis exclaimed. "Now listen carefully and I'll tell you what you're to do." Dāvids leaned forward on the sofa, nodding eagerly. "The arms are usually stolen from Nazi shipments, then they're distributed all over Latvia by the underground. We don't get many—maybe two or three dozens at a time. Most go to the underground in the eastern provinces. The guerrillas that get them from the trains are frequently known by the Nazis, so they have to stay in the background—in woods and marshes." Valdis grinned. "You ought to see them cover their tracks—experts, that's what they are! Anyway, we'll notify them about this cave. Whenever they get some guns for us, they'll go there the back way, through the marshes so they won't be seen. Then they'll notify headquarters—"

"Where's headquarters?" Dāvids asked.

Valdis shook his head. "Not even I know our local headquarters, and even if I did, I wouldn't tell you. The less you know, the safer for all concerned." He smiled half-apologetically. "Sorry, but that's the way it is. You won't even know when the guns are delivered to the cave until you're given a cue." Valdis looked sternly at Dāvids. "And you remember this—I don't want you going there to see if they've come. Understand?"

"Sure—it might arouse suspicion."

Valdis grinned in approval. "You're a smart one, Dāvid. Anyway, a different person each time usually—some nearby farmer as a rule—will notify you he needs peat. He'll use the word *indīgas*—poisonous—and he'll use it several times in the conversation. That's your key word. It means another load of guns have arrived at the cave, and you're to go there, get the guns, hide them under a load of peat, and deliver them to him—"

"Can't the farmer come to Dāvids to pick up the load?" Daila asked worriedly. "That way he—"

"Daila, my love, stop coddling your brother," Valdis said crossly. "He is sorely needed. He's the perfect camouflage. What Nazi will suspect a kid like him? He doesn't look much older than Kārlis, and he'd be the perfect foil. I don't like using children either. But this is war. I think Dāvids wants to do something." Dāvids nodded vigorously. "Besides, over the years your father always delivered his peat. Every farmer for miles around knows that. It was something he prided himself on—that he delivered a good load of peat at a fair price. We don't want to arouse suspicion now by having the farmer come to get his peat. Also, with that Bolshevik on the place, we couldn't unload what Dāvids brings from the bog onto another wagon without risking detection."

"How often do I do this?" Dāvids asked.

"Oh, probably once every three or four months —rarely oftener. We don't get guns that fast." He gave a wry smile. "So you see, the risk is minimal. But what you do is valuable beyond measure. And by the way, thanks for the money. They can use it!"

Dāvids went home happier than he'd been in weeks. And even if his role was minor, still it made him a part of the resistance movement.

As the weeks went by, the local radio news broadcasts were strangely noncommittal about German advances in Russia. Yet the Latvians who secretly listened to the forbidden short-wave radios spread the word; because of the vicious Russian winter that was setting in, the Nazis were in trouble and facing terrible setbacks in their drive to take Moscow. Locally, the Nazis were sending young Latvian men to the eastern province of Latgale to scout for Russian guerrillas and to provide a backup force.

In late October a farmer to the north called Dāvids on the telephone and ordered a load of peat. And he used the word *indīgas* several times.

"I'll deliver it Saturday," Dāvids said, feeling his heart race with excitement.

Saturday morning he harnessed Melnis and again Peter eyed him warily as he rode off. When he arrived at the peat bog he went directly to the cave. With a sense of great pride he lifted the sixteen rifles and the cartridges of ammunition and placed them in his wagon. They were the latest Nazi automatics. Then he began cutting peat, piling it atop the guns spread out over the bed of the wagon. When he reached the barn again, he could see Peter way out in the fields cutting grain. On a sudden inspiration, he pulled the wagon up by the barn and began loading manure atop the peat. Then he drove out onto the road.

He was almost at Vilis Mukins's farm when two Nazis approached him. "What've you got there?" demanded one of them.

Dāvids grinned. "Can't you smell it?"

"What's it for?"

"I'm delivering it to a farmer. He doesn't have any cows, and he wants to spread some manure over his vegetable garden so it can lie fallow till spring."

The two Nazis walked around the back and Dāvids fought to keep from stiffening. The smile stayed on his face, but it was as though it was there all by itself — frozen.

When one Nazi dug into the manure and saw the peat, he looked accusing at Dāvids. "So—you hide something?"

"No," Dāvids said with a calmness that surprised him. "I deliver manure and peat. Haven't you ever mixed the two for farming?" Then he shrugged. "No, I guess not. Only a farmer knows that peat and manure make the best bed for a garden." Suddenly he remembered Kārlis's irritating manner of piling questions one atop another, and how it always made everyone want to get away from him. "What did you do before you became soldiers? Did you live in a city? I never did. What's it like? What part of Germany are you from? What's it like there? What do they grow there? Do you have much snow? You know, we'll have snow soon." He barely gave them time to mumble an answer before another question popped out at them.

"Go deliver your smelly stuff," the Nazis finally said and waved him on.

Still hollering questions at them, Dāvids drove off,

beginning to whistle like a carefree farm kid delivering a stinky load of manure. But it was all he could do to keep his stiff mouth puckered into a whistle.

When he drove homeward at dusk, his whistle was truly one of joy. He had done his first job as an underground worker, and he'd done it well.

On the farm the first heavy snows of winter turned the countryside into a fairyland of wide expanses of white fields, their smoothness broken only by the footprints of a stray fox or deer. Tree limbs drooped with their weight of snow, and blue shadows were long because of the low sun.

In the two months since Dāvids had discovered the cave and made his first underground delivery, he had found nothing to implicate Peter further. Muddy boots could just as easily mean the marshes as the bog, he was forced to admit. And no more supplies had been missing. He realized he had been looking for something in Peter to pin his hate on, something to offset his grudging admiration that was growing for the strange, quiet man. So he'd grabbed at the cave and the missing vodka.

On November eighteenth, a new problem occupied Dāvids's thoughts. Not since the Russians had overrun their country had they been allowed to observe their national Independence Day openly. But Dāvids had ideas of his own. It was Tuesday, and the Nazis refused to allow the regular holiday, so all children had to go to school, and offices and factories were open. But after school, and after work, Daila, Valdis, and Oskars came to the house. Māmiņa, Daila, Marta, and Gunārs's wife, Elza, put on their native costumes of varicolored skirts topped with handloomed shawls, and they wore heirloom silver jewelry and amber beads. Daila, though married now, wore the crown-shaped headdress to represent the unmarried girl, while the others wore brightly colored kerchiefs. Verners, Rolfs, and Gunārs wore the full-sleeved blouses and embroidered vests, and Dāvids, Kārlis—his leg now healed—and the twins were clad in full trousers and shirts with embroidered cuffs. The living room was decorated with the crimson-white-crimson flags and boughs were tied in clusters on chairs and hung on the walls.

While Gunārs played his accordion, everyone danced the familiar waltzes and sang the "Dainas"—the folksongs. At first the singing was listless and uninspired, as though no one had much heart for it. But Dāvids persisted, and soon the Latvian's natural love of music and his hilarious enjoyment of the endless varieties of "Dainas" won out.

The table was set with plenty of food, and by evening everyone was lighthearted. Dāvids looked with quiet satisfaction at his mother's smiling face. An occasional clouding told that she missed Papus, but she seemed happier than he'd seen her in many months.

Peter had been invited, but he declined and stayed in his own cabin.

When the celebration ended and things were being carefully and lovingly packed away, Kārlis yanked down the Latvian flag.

"It's wrong—having this," he said and tossed it to the floor. "We shouldn't sing Latvian songs anymore. Our German teachers tell us we must sing songs of the Fatherland."

A dead, shocked silence greeted this statement. Then Rolfs snatched the flag off the floor and looked at the wide-eyed boy as though he ached to spank him.

"Your head's stuffed with the wrong things," he said tightly and walked away. Everyone began talking at once, berating Kārlis for his unpatriotic remarks while he looked confused.

Suddenly Dāvids walked over and put an arm across his shoulders, while he faced the angry people. "He's only mouthing what he hears," he reminded them. "How long has it been since we've done anything like this—except for Daila's wedding? All Kārlis knows is war—and Russians and Nazis." He remembered vividly how surprised his brother had been when seeing the bridal arbor.

That night when they were in bed, he told Kārlis, "Remember what Papus said? What goes on in this house is never to be mentioned to the Nazis. They want us to be like them. But we're Latvians, and we want to remember that." When Kārlis made no reply, Dāvids asked, "Don't you want to grow up and be like Papus?"

"Oh, yes," came the enthusiastic reply in the dark.

"Well, Papus was Latvian. Don't ever forget it, Kārli. And remember—say nothing to the Nazis."

"Why?"

"Because they might deport us—or even kill us."

He could hear Kārlis suck in his breath, and he hated frightening the child. Yet he didn't dare let Kārlis blab at school about their private Independence Day celebration. No telling how the Nazis would react to that.

"I won't tell," Kārlis said softly, "just like you didn't tell the Russians anything."

In an agony of guilt Dāvids turned to the wall. That night he had another nightmare.

The news from the front got worse. The Germans were bogged down in mud or immobilized by the bitter cold and the snow. Automatic weapons wouldn't function and soldiers suffered frostbite; or worse, they froze to death. Moscow had not been taken. In Latvia the Nazis were glum, though the propaganda blaring from the radios promised great military offenses in the spring. To add to the German worries were the persistent sabotaging of the local war-related industries. There were heavy-handed reprisals, but the subversive work continued. Strategic rail centers in Latgale Province—important in maintaining supply lines to the beleaguered Nazi soldiers in Russia—were consistently blown up. And the head of food supplies in Jelgava was killed by a sniper.

All of this troubled Dāvids. If the Germans were driven back, the Russians would return. Yet to help strengthen Germany meant contributing to domination by Hitler. They were caught in an impossible bind. Their only hope was help from the British, like in the First World War.

In February Dāvids turned fourteen, and partly to create interest and love of familiar customs in Kārlis, he insisted that his birthday be celebrated in the Latvian way with music, and even the old custom of the honoree being seated in a chair decorated with boughs. All the others, grasping the four legs of the chair, lifted it as much as they could. This time Peter joined in the evening celebration, and with his help, Gunārs and Verners were able to lift the chair, getting Dāvids at least a foot off the ground. Everyone cheered while Dāvids held on tightly to the precariously rocking chair, and Kārlis kept yelling, "Let me do it, let me do it."

Wiry little Gunārs, laughing so hard he lost his grip, couldn't keep his end up, and the chair tipped, sending Dāvids sliding to the floor.

"You've grown too much," Peter said as he helped him up.

While everyone teased him about growing—though actually he was still short for his age—Dāvids looked in wonder at Peter. It was the first time he'd ever seen Peter smile—though it certainly wasn't a face-creasing kind. Still—it was a smile—and it made Peter look almost human.

Winter gave way to spring and Dāvids got another *indīgas* call for peat. So on a Saturday morning he again got his load of guns and the peat. This time he didn't take manure since this particular farmer had cows, and therefore had his own manure. The delivery went without a hitch and Dāvids was paid for his peat. This payment Valdis had insisted on, saying it would prevent questions or suspicion. And Dāvids turned the money back to the underground.

Again Valdis praised him for his patriotism, and Dāvids's self-esteem—which often slipped into black depths of guilt and condemnation—rose to where he walked with head high.

Summer came, bringing the end of school, and also the seventeen-hour workday. A two-hour rest after lunch was essential, since everyone worked from five in the morning and would work again till after nine in the evening. The spring plantings were in, the cows had been let out of the barn and were giving more milk than required by the quotas, so Dāvids was able to sell considerable amounts of butter to the soldiers going through Latvia to the front. In Germany, according to the soldiers, it was hard to get and they couldn't buy enough of the sweet Latvian butter.

The hidden inventories varied at times, but Dāvids tried to keep a fair amount on hand. In the small leather bag in the attic trunk, he had a reasonable supply of marks—enough to make him congratulate himself as a farm manager. Though he knew he owed most of the success to Peter, still he felt he at least deserved credit for hanging onto the farm.

Then one June day a ham was missing, and Māmiņa denied taking it. In July a jar of honey disappeared. Then, just as they were about to sow the winter rye in August, five more cases of vodka, hidden in the grainery pit, were gone. Dāvids had counted it the day before; then when he went to get a case for Oskars, who had several Nazis interested in buying some, the five cases had disappeared overnight. Who around this farm could use up five cases of vodka without it being obvious? he wondered. It had to be that whoever took it sold it—or stored it elsewhere until it could be sold.

He remembered how Peter had seemed annoyed when he first went to the bog, and very curious when he returned. Could it be that Peter used the cave, too, to hide the vodka? Since Dāvids had never mentioned seeing the cave, maybe Peter figured he'd never noticed it and so used it, too. Certainly it wasn't visible from the new trail down to the peat. But this would never do. The risk of the vodka and the guns being there at the same time was too great.

Without saying where he was going, he saddled Berta. Once out of sight of the house, he turned and headed to the cave. But when he got there, it was exactly as it had been before. There were no cases of vodka hiding inside it—or any evidence that there ever had been. Not even a footstep around it.

Disappointed that he hadn't found what he had expected to find, he mounted Berta and headed toward home. Five cases of vodka simply couldn't disappear into thin air. Peter never went into town, so if he had to get rid of it, he would surely use such a place as the cave as a drop-off point. Gunārs didn't go into town often, and usually when he did, he rode a horse. And five cases of vodka—even one case—couldn't be hidden on a horse very easily. True, Verners went into town often to see a girl, but he, too, rode a horse. He sighed in perplexity.

He was still in the woods when he heard barking. It was Stulbenis—he'd know that noisy, frantic yapping anywhere. He grinned—the dog probably had a fox cornered, and he'd treed some animal. Dāvids put his fingers in his mouth to whistle for the dog, when suddenly a shot rang out—then another—followed immediately by the agonizing "yip yip" that said Stulbenis was hit!

Jabbing his heels into Berta's side, he galloped toward the sound. As he broke into a small clearing, he caught a glimpse of two men dashing into the woods beyond. They were afoot. His instant thought was that these men had come to the peat bog to pick up the five cases of vodka that had been put there for them.

"Stulbeni!" he cried out and heard a moan. Quickly he rode over to where the dog lay in a pool of blood. His bushy tail tried to wag as Dāvids dismounted and knelt by him. But when Dāvids reached out to touch him, Stulbenis bared his teeth and growled.

He had been shot in the hip and in the stomach, and Dāvids didn't dare try to lift him up into the saddle. Ignoring the growling, he stuffed grass against the leg wound to slow the bleeding, then he tied his kerchief around it. Next he wadded more grass against the stomach, peeling off his shirt to press also against the wound. All the while he murmured to the moaning dog.

"You'll be all right," he said with more assurance than he felt. "I'll go get a wagon. You wait here." Patting him, even as tears ran down his face, he pleaded, "Don't die, Stulbeni, don't die. I'll come right back."

He mounted Berta, but when he looked back, Stulbenis whined, looking as though he felt he was being deserted. "I'll come back," Dāvids sobbed and raced off, jabbing his heels into the horse's side.

When he arrived at the far end of the farm, none of the men were in the fields—only the twins out in the far pasture with the cows. So he raced toward the house. Out by the barn Peter was talking to the workers.

"Somebody get the wagon," Dāvids called and slid out of the saddle the minute he got close. "Stulbenis has been shot. He's dying."

At the first words Peter bolted to the shed and got the wagon as the others gathered around to hear what had happened.

"Russian guerrillas!" Māmiņa screeched, turning pale. "I've heard they sneak up to farms and demand food. Sometimes they kill the farm people."

"Oh Māmin, don't be so dramatic," Dāvids said irritably, noticing Kārlis's fearful look. Kārlis was just beginning to lose the timid expression he so often had, and Dāvids didn't want new terrors inflicted on the boy.

Peter brought the wagon out and hitched Melnis to it. Tossing some rags into the wagon, as well as the medicine kit used for all the animals, he mounted the wagon, with Dāvids scrambling up beside him.

"Get started on the seeding of the rye," Peter called out to the two men. "I'll be back as soon as I can. I want to get it in before it rains." Peter cast a wary eye at the clouds overhead.

Typical of Peter, he said nothing when Dāvids told him where the dog was, but he headed straight there. Even with concern over his dog, Dāvids wondered if Peter knew every inch of this farm—he certainly acted as though he did.

Stulbenis was still alive when they got to him, though

he was having trouble breathing. With his usual com-
petence, Peter bound the wounds and gently lifted
Stulbenis into the wagon. The dog growled, and even bit
Peter's wrist, but he was too weak to resist much.

"Will he die, Peter?" Dāvids asked as they got back onto the wagon.

"If he lives through the night—" Peter shrugged, as
though to say there might be a slim chance. Occasionally
he glanced back at the dog wrapped in an old tattered
blanket.

"Do you think they were Russian guerrillas?" Dāvids
asked after a while.

"Could be."

Dāvids looked at him in surprise. Somehow he had expected Peter to pooh-pooh such an idea, especially if he
had been the one delivering the vodka to the guerrillas.
"Doesn't it bother you?" he asked.

Peter nodded. "Of course it does. I'm a Russian deserter."

Dāvids gasped. He'd never realized that in the eyes of
the Russians, Peter would be considered a deserter. The
last person in the world he would want to contact would
be a guerrilla. But it was entirely possible that the
guerrilla was looking for Peter.

"Do you think they're looking for you?"

Peter shrugged.

"But you came over here," Dāvids persisted. "You
could be in danger." He looked straight at him. "Why,
Peter—why?"

"Your dog was hurt," was the simple reply, and Dāvids
knew somehow that Peter meant just exactly that. He was
loyal to them all—even to the dumb dog.

Again he felt shame wash over him. How could he have
suspected Peter? In all the months he'd been with them,

Peter had never once done anything truly suspicious. And he worked endless hours, for little pay, doing whatever had to be done without complaint. He had proven in countless ways his gratitude to the family who had given him shelter. As a deserter, Peter needed a place to hide, which probably explained why he never left the farm, except during *talka*, and then he merely went to the neighboring farms to work.

For two days, while Peter worked out in the fields, Dāvids and Kārlis watched over Stulbenis by day, hand-feeding him, and Peter took over at night. He kept the dog in his cabin. By the end of the second day it was clear Stulbenis would live, though he would always drag his hind leg.

A week after Stulbenis was shot, word came that two Latvian army deserters had been killed in the woods near Glūda. This answered Dāvids's curiosity as to who shot the dog. But the big question of who took the vodka was still unanswered.

CHAPTER 9

BY THE END of the year, people began to complain of lack, and those in the cities suffered the most. Coupons for food were issued, and prices continually climbed, while the black-market business soared. Coal was almost nonexistent. Only those living on farms fared better.

Though the farm yield was not as great as Dāvids would have liked, it was good. They had met their Nazi quotas and managed to set aside several hams and sides of bacon, over and above their own needs. And a cigarette shortage during November enabled them to sell their hidden supplies at good prices. Also, two more shipments of *indīgas* peat brought in money for the underground.

Dāvids made a consistent effort to woo Kārlis away from his Nazi leanings, and frequently when walking home from school on a cold cloudy day, they would sing "Dainas." On Māmiņa's name day in October, they decorated the house, sang songs to her, and presented her with three beautiful yellow chrysanthemums from a bush they had especially singled out of the flower bed and had pruned just so, in order to have these perfect blooms. Again in November they held their own private Independence Day celebration, and this time Kārlis heartily joined in.

At Christmastime they decorated a tree, sang the traditional songs, and had the delicious sweet breads that made the holiday so special. Dāvids had noticed that Kārlis frequently sketched pictures on scraps of paper, so as a gift he gave him a drawing pad and several soft-leaded art pencils.

"Let's make this a Latvian book," he told Kārlis. "See how many pictures you can draw that depict our Latvian life." And Kārlis, delighted with his gift, surprised everyone with his talent as he drew pictures of animals, birds, the farm, the clouds, and everyone on the farm.

There were no peat deliveries throughout the winter —it would be too hard to get it from under the load of snow—but after Valdis had been sent to Latgale in January, Dāvids visited Daila as often as possible, helping her print anti-Nazi leaflets in the basement of her little house. These were distributed throughout the area by others and were aimed at keeping the local Latvians apprised of atrocities and arrests by the soldiers and the Gestapo. This inflamed the people, lending fire to the resistance movement.

"They're small things—what we do," Daila said one day when Dāvids complained of wanting to take a more active part in the resistance, "but they're effective—and necessary. It constantly saps the Nazis' attention at a time when they desperately want to devote all their time to the Russian effort."

Dāvids was forced to go along with her suggestion. Life under Nazi domination was harsh, but out on the farm life seemed to go along fairly smoothly. Māmiņa still showed little interest in the farm, and Oskars came out when he could, though the excessive demands of the brick factory kept him away. The senseless slaughter of one of Kārlis's classmates had finally turned him away from any respect for Naziism, and he spent long hours drawing pictures. Stulbenis was as noisy and dumb as ever, though he dragged a hind leg. Daila went to work as secretary at the brick factory, so Dāvids could visit her to print leaflets only on Saturdays or Sundays.

Even the hired help seemed content to stay. Verners was courting a girl in Glūda, and Gunārs's family frequently had friends visit them at their cabin on Sunday. Even Peter seemed less glum.

There was only one flaw in Dāvids's smoothly running farm life. Every so often food was still missing—a ham, some butter, a case of vodka, and a carton or two of cigarettes—never any great amount, but a steady draining. He was sure Peter wasn't involved, yet he didn't know who to blame. He tried posting a watch, but he'd never seen anyone taking the stuff. Whoever was doing it knew when he was away, so it had to be someone on the farm.

In February Dāvids turned fifteen—a little taller now and with an assurance that belied his youthful appearance. Māmiņa sent him out to get a bottle of vodka for the big celebration they would have, since it was Sunday and Oskars and Daila were coming to dinner. Being it was a party, all the hired hands were invited, too.

Singing joyously, he headed to the grainery. As he passed the closed barn, he heard a sound and paused in his singing. It was Peter—crooning in Russian. It was the first time Dāvids had ever heard Peter sing—albeit a sad song.

He smiled to himself. Peter was happiest when doing farm work. His singing proved he didn't even mind being in the barn in winter—something Dāvids avoided if he could. Because winters were severe, the cows were kept in the barn from November until May. Naturally, manure accumulated. Regularly a layer of fresh straw was laid over it, and as the months went by, the pile got higher and higher. Even the feeding and watering troughs had to be raised by chains and pulleys. The massive pile of manure generated a lot of heat, which warmed the barns. In May the animals would be let out, then there would be a *talka*, and all the manure would be spread out in the fields as fertilizer. It was Dāvids's least favorite job. In the meantime, by February and March, the barn was a powerfully stinking place. Though Dāvids normally loved everything about his farm, and generally never even noticed the smell of manure because it was an inherent part of any farm, for some reason he found the closed barn too strong and he avoided it, if possible. Yet here was Peter—singing! Dāvids's curiosity about the big black-haired man was as strong as ever—but Peter was as closemouthed about himself as always.

Dāvids continued to the grainery, shoved aside the bags of grain, lifted the lid to the pit—and stared in disbelief. It was empty! All nine cases gone! Fury boiled up inside him. Someone on the place was disloyal, and he was going to find out who. He'd checked this pit only a week ago. He turned and started to stomp out, determined to confront them all—right now! Then he paused. No, that wouldn't be the way. Whoever was doing it would lie. Certainly no one would blatantly confess.

From another pit he removed one bottle of vodka from a case, covered the pit and walked back to the house, forcing himself to appear cheerful and calm. After all, today was his birthday. They would expect him to be singing—on top of the world.

It was a happy party and it lasted late into the night. Gifts were hard to buy these days, but Māmiņa had knitted him a new blue-and-white scarf, and Daila had made mittens. Kārlis painted a picture showing the farm in winter, and around the border were drawings of small Latvian flags intertwined with myrtle boughs. As usual none of the help gave gifts, but Oskars presented him with a safety razor, which brought forth much teasing. Though Dāvids's beard was still sparse, he liked owning his own razor.

A few days later, at bedtime, Stulbenis was not inside, and Dāvids went to the back door to call him. A cold north wind whined through the bare branches of the tree in the backyard and he debated whether merely to whistle for him or go down to Peter's cabin, since Stulbenis frequently visited Peter in the evening. Since Kārlis had been in one of his incessant-question moods tonight, and Māmiņa was out of sorts, the peace and silence of Peter's presence seemed most welcome, and Dāvids decided to go down and see him, using the excuse he'd come for his dog.

Outside, the night was black, and as he passed the smokehouse, shivering because he had not put on his heavy coat, he saw a glimmer of moving light shine from under the door, as though someone had a flashlight. Suddenly there was darkness, and the door opened. Dāvids couldn't see who it was—only that the vague shadow headed toward the cabins. Silently he followed in the snow, his heart pounding, partly in excitement because he was sure he'd come upon the thief, and partly in a kind of fear. If it was Peter—could he face that silent, impassive man and accuse him? And if it was

Peter—would he have to send him away? This, he realized, he didn't want to do. He was reluctant to admit it, but he liked Peter—and he needed him on the farm.

The cold wind cut through his sweater, and he clamped his teeth shut so they wouldn't chatter and give his presence away. No lights were visible at either cabin—sitting side by side away from the other buildings—because of the wartime blackout. The shadowy figure continued toward the cabins, and suddenly the door to one opened, the figure stepped inside, and immediately the door closed. In the momentary light of the open door, Dāvids recognized the thief—and the ham under his arm. It was the wiry little man—Gunārs.

In a rage of indignation, he had only one thought—catch him with the goods before he could hide it. Charging up the two steps, he yanked open the door and stepped inside. Gunārs, reaching out his hands to warm them at the stove, spun around and jumped in front of the kitchen table. Elza gave a squeak of fright and stuffed a fist in her mouth.

"So!" Dāvids raged at him and shoved him aside. The ham was clearly visible on the table. "You're the one who's been stealing from me. What's the matter, don't we give you enough to eat?"

"I—I—" Gunārs looked at his wife for help, but she continued to stare wide-eyed with fear. "No, I've never stolen anything," he said. "I—I—was going to buy this from you tomorrow. M-my parents, in town, need food."

"You lie!" Dāvids threw at him. "If you had wanted that tomorrow, you could've asked me for it then. But you stole it—just like you've stolen bacon and vodka—"

"I—I took only a little vodka—"

"A little! You could get half of Latvia drunk on what you stole!"

"What's going on here?" came Peter's deep voice from behind him. Evidently he'd heard the commotion from the next cabin.

"This—this—louse—this traitor—" Dāvids was almost incoherent with indignation as he pointed to the frightened Gunārs. "He's been stealing me blind for a year."

"No—just a few things—" Gunārs protested.

Peter started to speak, but Dāvids cut in. "What did you do with them?"

Gunārs merely shrugged.

Suddenly Dāvids remembered the numerous visitors coming on Sundays to Gunārs's cabin. Many of them came in wagons. It would be a simple matter for them to carry away the stolen items. Gunārs was probably running a black market of his own—with Dāvids's supplies!

Dāvids spun on Peter. "You live right next to him. Did you know what he was doing?"

"I suspected."

"And you didn't tell me!"

"I had no proof."

Dāvids elbowed Gunārs aside and snatched up the ham. "Well, I do," he snarled, waving it at Peter. "All the proof I need." He spun on Gunārs. "You—get out—get your family out—now!"

"At night?" Elza cried out. "It's stormy—"

"Dāvid, wait till morning," Peter spoke up.

"You stay out of this," Dāvids yelled at him. "I won't have him on my farm. We've paid him a decent wage, and he eats well—better than those in town. We've even kept him here during the winter when there isn't much work. But no, he had to rob me. Well, let him go to one of his friends—the ones who've carted off my stuff." He

turned to Gunārs, his eyes blazing, his jaw set in stubbornness, and his legs spraddled as he hunched in a
fighting mood. He looked like an angry bulldog. "Now
get off my farm. You can come back later and get your
stuff. Go on—get—all of you!"

Mumbling threats, Gunārs and Elza headed to the
bedroom to wake the sleeping boys and get them dressed
for the cold ride to Glūda.

"Dāvid—don't let anger cloud your thinking," Peter
said calmly.

"I didn't ask for your advice," Dāvids snapped. He took
the ham and stormed out the door. "And send my dog
home," he yelled as he walked out.

A short time later he heard Gunārs's creaky old wagon
head down the lane. He felt no compassion that it was a
stormy night—Gunārs should have thought about the
consequences before he stole the ham.

The next morning at breakfast he was aware of Peter's
disapproval, but he ignored it, and even before the sky
was light, he and Kārlis headed up the road to school.

When classes were ended, Māmiņa was waiting outside
with the wagon. Kārlis was with her, having gotten out of
his elementary school a few minutes before.

"Anything wrong?" Dāvids asked, climbing up onto the
seat. It was rare that Māmiņa ever came for them.

"No, not really. Oskars phoned me this morning and
said Daila didn't show up at work," Māmiņa explained.
"So I called her and she was sick. After lunch I drove in
to see her." Māmiņa smiled, and her cheeks, apple red
from the intense cold, together with the softness of her
smile, made her look like Dāvids had remembered her
before Papus left—young and pretty. "I took her some
freshly baked rye bread, some potatoes from the cellar,

some jam, and a pork roast. That silly girl hasn't eaten properly. That's all that's wrong with her—she's half starved—sending food packages to Valdis all the time."

Then the smile vanished. "As I was coming into town, I passed Gunārs coming out for his belongings. Oh, Dāvids, he was so angry. He yelled, 'I'll get even with you for this.' He scares me."

"Gunārs is like Stulbenis—all noise, Māmin," Dāvids consoled her to keep her from worrying. After a while he began singing softly, and soon both Māmiņa and Kārlis joined him, and once again a smile came to her face as she sat bundled in her fur robe.

When Melnis turned the wagon off the road and down the lane that crossed the pasture, all singing ceased. Māmiņa gave a squeak of terror and her face paled, leaving the two spots in her cheeks glowing like daubs of paint.

"Dāvid—what's that car doing at our house?" Kārlis piped up, beginning to shiver. "It looks like the one that comes to our school when the Nazis ask questions. Is it the Gestapo, Dāvid?" He hiccuped. "What do they want? I haven't told them anything—honest, I haven't." His voice verged on hysteria. "Will they kill us—will they?"

"Kārli, shut up," Dāvids said through stiff lips. He was as afraid as his brother, but he didn't dare show it. Flicking the reins, he made Melnis trot faster.

An officer in a brown uniform, black boots, and a holstered gun, his hair shaved close on the sides of his head like most of the German soldiers, came out of the house as the wagon stopped near the shed.

"Heil Hitler!" he called out, snapping his arm upward.

"Heil Hitler," came Dāvids's reluctant reply. To Māmiņa and Kārlis he hissed, "Say nothing, either of you." In their hysteria they could disclose too much. "I'll do the talking." In a loud, angry voice he demanded of the officer, "What're you doing in my house?"

"Searching," came the calm reply.

Dāvids forced his face to remain expressionless as he jumped down and confronted the man defiantly, though his heart flipped over in cold fear. "Searching for what?"

"Contraband." The officer turned to several men coming out of the smokehouse with a ham and a side of bacon. "Put those here on the porch. Go check the other buildings."

"What makes you think we have contraband?" Dāvids demanded.

"A man — Gunārs Dravnieks — he reported to us that you have great quantities of contraband —"

"He lies!" Dāvids stormed. "He stole one of my hams and I fired him. Now he lies —"

"We'll see if he lies," the officer said coldly and walked away, cutting off further conversation.

"Go inside," Dāvids said in a low voice as he helped Māmiņa out of the wagon. "It's too cold out here for you. He won't find anything. And don't look so scared," he added to Kārlis. "Remember what Papus said once — they don't always know everything — and they like to scare information out of people. Now go inside, and, Māmiņ, you make some hot tea. It'd do you both good. Help calm you." He led them to the back door. "I'll stay here and keep an eye on them."

He followed the men into the grainery, and when they opened the door Stulbenis charged out, barking furiously.

"Stulbeni — shut up!" Dāvids yelled and grabbed the muzzle to silence him. It took all his self-control to keep an impassive face as they entered the grainery and shoved the bags of grain aside. Then he stared stupidly at the pits—the covers were gone, and in the pits was nothing but loose grain! The men reached their hands down into them, feeling for contraband, but they found nothing.

"What're these holes for?" the officer demanded.

Thinking quickly, Dāvids replied. "Just what you see—to catch any loose grain from leaks or broken bags. Makes it easier to gather."

"You have an awful lot of grain." It was an accusation.

"Of course we do—we have quotas to fill. It's stored here, by order of the Nazi agriculture depart—"

"Hmph," was the only reply.

Again and again the men searched, while Dāvids locked the dog in the shed, where he continued to bark. The men went from building to building, and each time Dāvids waited in agony for a hiding place to be discovered. The men found several crocks of butter, two jars of honey, three jars of gooseberry jam, some dried squash and dried mushrooms. Nothing more.

As though unable to comprehend what had happened, Dāvids followed numbly. Where was everything? Then he went cold with dread. Gunārs had come here while Māmiņa was away—and he'd taken everything. But where was Peter when this was going on? In fact, where was Peter now?

The officer opened the door to the barn and stepped back. "God! What a stink!"

"That's manure. The barn's full of it," Dāvids explained. "It'll be emptied out in the spring."

"Go in and search," the officer ordered his men.

Reluctantly they entered, while from the shed came the frantic barking as Stulbenis threw himself against the door time and time again. In a minute or two the men came out, hands over their noses. "Nobody would hide *anything* in here," one pale-faced one said, gasping for fresh air. "They'd never be able to sell it—or use it for anything."

"There's nothing but cows," said another, "and the biggest mound of manure I've ever seen."

"I told you," Dāvids said blandly, "that we run a proper farm."

The officer was clearly annoyed at finding no contraband, and he stomped back to the car. "Bring the food," he ordered his men.

"But we need—" Dāvids protested.

"Leave the squash and mushrooms," the officer said, then gave a leering smile. "The rest is our payment—for not turning you in."

Dāvids choked on his rage. It was blackmail—pure and simple! If he refused to give it to them, the officer would arrest him on a trumped-up charge. He nodded in defeat. Between Gunārs and the Nazis, he'd been stripped clean.

Just then Stulbenis succeeded in forcing the shed door open and he charged the men, yapping shrilly. A shot rang out and the dog dropped in his tracks—dead with a bullet in the head.

"You—you murderer!" Dāvids screamed as the officer sheathed his gun. "You stinking, filthy murderer!" He threw himself at the man, but the others grabbed him and flung him to the ground. Getting into the car with the food, they drove off. "You dirty cowards—you yellow-livered Huns!" Dāvids screamed after them, then he burst into tears as he cradled his dead dog.

CHAPTER 10

AT SCHOOL the next morning Dāvids found it almost impossible to listen to the usual propaganda of the supremacy of the German race without bellowing out his contempt, without telling his classmates how cowardly, how deceitful and vicious the Nazis were. But they were all aware of it, he knew. Amost every Latvian family had run up against Nazi doublecrossing and deceit in some way.

The classroom door opened and a man entered. His whole bearing shouted "Gestapo."

"Heil Hitler!" came the salute. "I have come for Dāvids Ozols."

Dāvids sat frozen in his seat as a murmur of shock and curiosity rippled through the room. Somehow the Gestapo must have learned about his underground activities. The punishment was death—but he knew the Gestapo would try to torture information out of him first. The memory of the NKVD beating and the rumors of Gestapo torture tactics tied his stomach in knots.

Then on shaking legs he rose slowly. Moving like a robot without emotion or expression, he followed the man. He made a valiant effort to stride out defiantly, head high, but inwardly he was lost—in despair. His numbed brain delivered only one message—I will not break under torture. He would not weaken and admit Daila or Valdis were involved. His greatest fear was that Daila might already be arrested.

In the car he sat stiffly beside the unsmiling man. His legs felt heavy, like logs, and it was hard to breathe because his chest was constricted. He longed to get out and walk, to still the restlessness, to ease the tightness. Instead he sat with ice cold hands folded in his lap, trying to force his mind away from the torture to come.

A half hour later he stood in a large room facing several men—one who seemed to be the judge. With a faint sigh of relief he realized Daila was not there. The silence dragged on, so reminiscent of the NKVD questioning. Only the tapping pencil was missing.

A door at the left opened and Gunārs and Elza entered, looking smug. So great was Dāvids's relief that he almost laughed aloud. He wasn't arrested because of gun smuggling, but because this foolish man had a complaint. The dread he had been feeling turned immediately into intense anger. How dare this idiot drag him here like this? A look of determination showed in the set of his jaw.

The officer who had killed Stulbenis entered and the usual "Heil Hitler" salute was given, followed by a period of questioning. Gunārs told of the cases of vodka and the cartons of cigarettes in hiding—of jars of honey and the other items. Then the officer reluctantly admitted that he had found nothing. He stated that he had returned again this morning and thoroughly searched, even going down to the marshes, but he had found nothing. Dāvids could see he was disappointed not to be able to verify Gunārs's story.

"What little we had was for our own private use," Dāvids said calmly, "and he stole it. I caught him the other night taking a ham. We're entitled to vodka and cigarettes—we're given coupons each month as part payment for our produce—especially our milk. You can check with the creamery—"

"I already have," the judge cut in icily. He turned to Gunārs. "Did you take a ham?"

"Er—well, we wanted to buy—" All smugness fled.

"Did you ever take anything else?"

"Y-yes—in a way—"

"And did you sell it?"

Desperation made his voice quiver. "We needed m-money for emer—"

"You are a thief—stealing from your employer and selling it in the black market," the judge intoned in a bored manner. Then he added the sentence in a monotone while he looked out a window, as though he had repeated these same words a hundred times. "For that you will be sent to Germany, to work in a munitions facto—"

"But my wife—my two little children—" Gunārs wailed. "What will happen—?"

"I'm not concerned with your problems," came the indifferent reply. "Let her go live with her parents. Get your things packed—you will leave next Wednesday." He flicked his wrist, dismissing Gunārs.

It happened so quickly that Dāvids stood rooted in amazement. This was Nazi justice—a fair trial? He couldn't feel justification that Gunārs had gotten what he deserved, so shaken was he by the manner in which the trial was conducted.

As two men began to lead Gunārs from the room, he yelled, "Wait! I'll tell you about him. Ask him about his peat bog—ask him if the Nazis know of it. Ask him if he shares the proceeds of it." He leered at Dāvids as he strained forward—hate distorting his face. "Go on—ask him!"

Fear turned Dāvids's legs to rubber, and it took all his self-control to maintain his poise. But he couldn't keep his heart from leaping into his throat, making it hard to breathe. How much did Gunārs know? He caught a glimpse of the officer, a malevolent glint coming into his eyes. Gunārs had been sentenced to slave labor and no obvious punishment had been given to Dāvids who had insulted him, calling him a yellow-livered Hun. Now he gloated at the turn of events and it was clear he knew Dāvids was afraid.

"Well?" the judge demanded of Dāvids. "*Do* you have a peat bog?" Dāvids nodded. "And you sell the peat?"

"Only occasionally."

"And you pocket the money?"

"Yes—to pay salaries—" he lied as he threw a hateful look at Gunārs, "including *his* pay. I—"

With a jerk of his head the judge dismissed Gunārs and Elza. "Take them out," he ordered, and the two —wailing and protesting the harsh sentence—were led away.

The judge then looked down at a sheaf of papers on his desk. "He is too young for Germany," he said wearily, as though bored with it all. "But we can use him in the prisoner-of-war camp near Tukums." He glanced up with cold eyes. "You'll serve there as an orderly for fifteen months. Be at the railroad station at Glūda in five days. Now get out. Heil Hitler."

Dāvids was numb as the heavy door slammed behind him. He was being sent from his beloved farm. But even worse—he wouldn't be able to help with the underground. He felt almost as though he had betrayed them. Tukums was not more than forty kilometers away, but it might as well be across the continent. He would practically be a prisoner-of-war himself. Fifteen months! It seemed like eternity.

Dazed, he shuffled past the country store and felt a stab of guilt, remembering Jēkabs. He shuddered, thinking of where he would have to go—to live among miserable, mistreated prisoners. He'd heard about the terrible conditions at these prison camps.

Yet even as desolation overcame him, there was one glimmer of satisfaction. They had not known about his underground work. He had not betrayed the others.

As he walked toward Kārlis's school, he wondered what had happened to Peter. The only explanation was that he had seen the Nazis coming and had taken off. But surely he hadn't been able to take much in the way of supplies. He felt disappointed in Peter. It wasn't like him to desert them. Yet at breakfast this morning he was still missing.

Putting Peter out of his thoughts, he reached Kārlis's school and explained to the authorities that his mother was ill so the teacher would release the boy. All the way home he tried to think how to tell Māmiņa what had happened. She would go into shock, or cry and carry on, or worst of all, she'd say, "I'll give up the farm and move to town." She wouldn't realize that in her condition it would be hard to get a job paying a decent salary. At least on the farm she ate—in town she would really suffer. But it was impossible to make her understand this. Even seeing the conditions under which Oskars—and Daila—lived, didn't seem to register on her mind.

"What's wrong, Dāvid?" Kārlis asked as they plodded home in a light snowfall. "How come those men killed Stulbenis? What'd they want anyway? Are you scared, Dāvid—are you? I am."

The usual "Shut up, Kārli," was on Dāvids's tongue. But suddenly he realized Kārlis's incessant questioning was a nervous reaction to stress. No one ever bothered to tell him what was going on—consequently his fears created problems greater than they were sometimes. So he explained what had happened. As he spoke, he wondered if it would be possible for Kārlis to carry on, delivering the peat. After all, he was nine now.

"What'll happen here at the farm—with you gone?" Kārlis asked fearfully.

"I don't know. If Peter were here, I'd have him run it. But he's gone." He shook his head wearily. "I don't know, Kārli. I simply don't know."

"He's a spy—Peter, I mean."

"Oh Kārli—grow up!" Dāvids said and sighed. He was in no mood for spy games. But he knew now that he could never tell Kārlis about the hidden guns. His fears would give him away, and his vivid imagination would force him to tell somebody.

When they reached the farm, all Dāvids's despair fled as he saw Peter heading to his own cabin. Quickly he raced over.

"Where *were* you?" he demanded, overcome with relief.

"In the barn." Peter opened the door and stepped inside.

Stomping snow off his boots, Dāvids followed. "You mean—when the man came searching?" Peter nodded. "And last night and this morning?" Again Peter nodded.

"Until I was sure it was safe," he added dryly.

"And all the supplies—did Gunārs take them?" Dāvids continued.

"No. I did."

"Where are they?"

"Buried in manure."

Dāvids burst into laughter, remembering the reactions when the men entered the barn. Then he quickly sobered. "Ye gods, Peter—only the vodka will be any good now. All the rest—cigarettes—food—that stink will ruin them—"

"Not if they're sealed in milk cans." Peter put a kettle of water on the stove. Glancing at Dāvids, he said non-committally, "You look worried."

"I'm being sent to the prison camp at Tukums for fifteen months." Groaning, he added, "Fifteen months, Peter—fifteen months is like a lifetime. I don't think I can stand it."

"Why are you being sent there?"

"Gunārs." He explained about Gunārs's sentence and his exposure of the existence of the peat bog. He straddled a chair near the wood stove. "Peter, how come you hid the stuff in the first place—how'd you know the Nazis would come?"

"I figured they might—knowing Gunārs."

Dāvids looked down. "You were right—as usual. I shouldn't have let my temper get the best of me."

"Takes time to learn lessons," was all Peter said and placed two tea mugs on the table.

"Will you run the farm for me, Peter?" Dāvids asked after a while. When Peter nodded, he gave a deep sigh of relief. The Nazis had found nothing wrong on the farm—thanks to Peter's quick thinking—and the quotas had always been met, so they probably would not bother anyone here too often. The peat bog wouldn't be used anymore. And with all their supplies intact, the family would be in a pretty good condition.

When he told Māmiņa later on, she accepted the news with almost detached calm, and as much as it worried him, knowing it wasn't a healthy sign, still he didn't want hysterics. And Māmiņa usually wavered between the two extremes.

The next morning Peter did not come to breakfast, nor was he at his cabin. Dāvids saddled Melnis and rode into Glūda to do a job he was reluctant to do—tell Daila about his fifteen-month sentence. But she'd heard the news from Māmiņa and she was amazingly calm. "We're lucky that they didn't learn about the smuggling," she said matter-of-factly. "But we'll have to find another place." She smiled, sliding an arm across his shoulder. "Frankly, I'm relieved. I never did feel comfortable having you deliver the stuff. But it sure did help a lot." She hugged him in sisterly approval. "You did a fine job, Dāvid. Valdis was impressed with the way you handled any encounter that you had with a Nazi."

Dāvids grinned warmly at her. For someone who still looked like a schoolgirl, she had a lot of stamina. She said she would continue printing the leaflets. "I'm going to have passports made for each of us," she added.

"Passports? Why—where are we going?"

Daila shrugged. "One never knows—but while I have someone who can forge passports, I'm going to get them."

Dāvids nodded. She was as stubborn as he was. But he knew one thing—he wasn't about to leave Latvia.

When he got home, Māmiŋa and Kārlis were in a state of panic. The Nazis had returned and had forced Rolfs to take them in the wagon to the peat bog. They had not returned. Again Dāvids felt the tightness in his chest. If they found the cave, they would suspect something. He would surely be questioned. And once again he envisioned himself in the Gestapo headquarters being beaten.

But when they returned an hour later, the officer looked coldly at him. "Where were you?" he demanded after the usual salute.

"I went to visit my sister — to tell her of my sentence."

"The bog isn't very big," the man admitted reluctantly. "But you're not to sell any of the peat without a permit." Again came the salute and the officer got into the car. In a moment they drove down the lane to the road.

Stunned by the unexpected outcome, Dāvids stared blankly at Rolfs getting slowly off the wagon. "Did they — did they inspect the bog carefully?" he asked.

"I guess they did," Rolfs replied. "We drove up to the place, and they sat on the wagon looking it over a long time."

Dāvids nodded, relieved. From where they would come out upon the bog, the cave wasn't visible. Evidently all they had wanted to see was whether there *was* a peat bog, and how large it might be. Obviously they had not considered it big enough to be important.

Later he saw Peter around and grinned to himself. Peter had an instinctive knowledge of when Nazis were coming. He'd probably guessed they would want to inspect the bog, so he'd hidden until they were gone.

The week went by, and Oskars tried every way to buy Dāvids's release or go in his place, all to no avail. So the fifth day at dawn Dāvids said good-bye to Peter, Māmiņa, and Kārlis on the farm. He didn't want any tearful farewells at the train station. Verners drove him to the depot, then solemnly shook his hand. Oskars and Daila showed up, bid him farewell, and then had to hurry to work. Finally, along with a carload of others—either too young, too old, or too feeble to serve in Germany—Dāvids boarded the train and was taken to Tukums.

The prison camp had once been an agricultural college, then a barracks for soldiers until it had been bombed. Now parts of it were still gutted, and the rest was a cold, cheerless collection of dreary buildings with bars at the windows, surrounded by farmland that was enclosed by high chain link fences topped with electrically charged coils of barbed wire. At strategic places, guard towers provided further deterrents to escape. Within the fence, about one hundred police ruled with harsh brutality, and about one thousand prisoners—mostly Russian—spent long, lonely hours waiting for spring, when at least they could work in the fields, planting potatoes.

All this Dāvids learned in his first hour there, and also that he was assigned to Building Four—a small complex that housed fifty prisoners—all Russians. It would be his job as orderly to clean the ten cells daily with disinfectant, feed those too sick to feed themselves—usually because they'd been taken to Interrogation and beaten—and in general take care of the needs of the others recovering from such treatment.

Sometimes there might be only one or two of his charges in a state needing his ministrations, and at other times there would be many. As the weeks went by, life for him was almost as bleak as it was for his prisoners—except that he wasn't subjected to interrogations and the vicious beatings. He was, however, under the authority of a sadistic officer who delighted in striking him with a riding crop if he was displeased, or kicking his shins. Dāvids slept in a cold, damp barracks on a bunk along with other 'workers' like himself. He showered in an unheated room with tepid water and ate tasteless stews, ersatz coffee that tasted like scrapings off the floor, and rye bread without butter.

His 'patients' were mostly emaciated, hollow-eyed men who shuffled about like robots. When one died or was transferred, another filled his place, so each of the ten cells was always filled with five men.

He paid little attention to their conversations. Most of it was filled with hate—with a desire for revenge, to 'get even' with whoever was responsible for their being captured and imprisoned. Most of the men here were officers in the Russian army—and those higher up in the Russian police system—cold-blooded, cruel men who, even when imprisoned and beaten, lived for the day they could someday retaliate even more brutally than before. Only a few prisoners were mere soldiers, unfortunate to be taken along with a high-ranking officer.

He did only what was required, and other than feed the weak ones, he ignored them as much as possible, feeling no compassion. All his hate for the Bolshevik was rekindled, and a return of the nightmares only intensified his feelings.

Letters from home—usually fairly dull because of the strict censorship—were all that made life tolerable as month after month passed. Māmiņa wrote that on Easter they had the usual celebration. Because she knew the letter would first be read by the authorities, that was all she said about Easter, but as Dāvids sat slumped on a bench, staring at the men shuffling about, getting their exercise in the great hall, he pictured Easter when he had been small and Papus was home. They would have a contest with their decorated eggs, each tapping the end of a hard-cooked colored egg against the end of another's. Amid lots of laughing and teasing, and trying every trick to break the other egg but not your own, the game went on. Also part of Easter were the swings—built especially high, just for the celebration, with their long ropes entwined with greenery. The idea was to see how high you could swing. To be able to soar upward high enough so the rope "snapped" before it dropped downward again was the sign of a good swinger. It was dangerous—but that was what made it exciting.

Every few weeks Kārlis sent him a picture—usually a pen-and-ink sketch, each one of some part of the farm —harmless little scenes that could pass inspection—the barn, the windmill, the marshes, even one of the day in May when the cows were first let out of the barn. He had captured the feeling—the way the usually staid, dull animals gamboled about like frisky calves, kicking up their heels, racing across the pastures, happy to be free again. The pictures brought the pain of nostalgia, but Dāvids treasured every one. It was like a little visit home each time one arrived.

Summer came and the prisoners now spent long hours out in the fields, using only the most primitive tools. The stronger ones seemed happier being busy, but the weak ones collapsed, and it was Dāvids's job to get them back on their feet. If they were unable to, he hauled them back to their cells.

He understood now a little how Māmiņa felt, living on the farm without Papus. She did all the usual things but with a kind of detachment. And that was how he felt about the prison. He worked, he fed the sick prisoners, he scrubbed cells, he occasionally got punished for insubordination, and once he was brutally beaten for failing to lock an outside door and four prisoners temporarily escaped. All this he bore with the same kind of detachment. His heart was at the farm, and at the end of the fifteen months he would return. In the meantime he lived for letters from home—especially for Kārlis's pictures.

The fall season was short, and winter came quickly, and once again the men were confined to Building Four—unable to go outdoors. Time dragged interminably to Dāvids, and he dreamed of home—longing to be there for Christmas. Then on December twentieth he was called to the office.

"You have been granted a two-week pass to go to your farm," he was told and the man behind the desk handed him an official paper covered with impressive stamps. "If you hurry, you can catch the one-o'clock train to Glūda. But remember—this pass allows you to go only to your home—nowhere else. And be back here on time."

Dāvids was speechless. A two-week pass! It was unheard of. Then he thought of Oskars—quiet, shy, conniving Oskars—and he wondered what items of scarce food had won this special treatment. He was at the station in time, and by two o'clock he arrived in Glūda and called Daila at work.

"Daila—it's me! I'm here at the railroad station. I'm going home—home!" he exclaimed, bubbling with excitement. "Can you take me there in your wagon as soon as you get off work?"

After crying in joy and saying how pleased she was, Daila told him, "Valdis has a leave, too, and he's due home tonight or tomorrow. But take my sleigh and go on out. I want to wait for him. Valdis and I will come later with Oskars." She sounded happy. "Oh, Dāvid, what a great Christmas this will be! I'll call Māmiņa and tell her you're coming."

Dāvids walked to her house, keeping a wary eye on the stormy sky. A frigid Arctic wind was blowing, and he pulled his greatcoat tighter as he plowed through the deep snow. In the shed behind her house he found the big wooden sleigh. Berta, the gray horse, was there. Evidently Māmiņa had give her to Daila to use when visiting the farm. He found a heavy blanket in the sleigh and wrapped it around his legs. Then with coat, cap, mittens, and scarf all pulled tight, he headed homeward. The snow was falling hard now, drifting up against the packed snow already deep upon the ground.

By the time he got out of Glūda, heading home, he knew this was no ordinary storm — it was the beginning of a blizzard! Though he would have preferred Melnis in a situation like this, still Berta was a strong horse.

The sky darkened, and the wind rose, howling and wailing till it sounded to him like wolves baying at a full moon. The thick snow swirled about so that he couldn't see too far ahead, and even the trees lining the road disappeared into a fog.

The little white painted posts that lined the road disappeared under drifts and he couldn't tell where the road was. He was out in open flatland, where fields, horizon, and sky blended into the same whiteness — a whiteness that blew into his eyes with stinging intensity. He huddled down into his coat, and tucked the blanket tighter around his legs, but the icy wind cut through him as though he was naked. He couldn't even use trees to tell where the road was, because the weight of snow burdened the limbs, and what might have been a corridor in a forest was now just a tangle of limbs.

Berta wanted a warm barn, and she charged through the drifts with her usual unpredictable recklessness, so that the sleigh slid and bounced and slued around dangerously. Pulling on the reins did no good. All Dāvids could do was hang on with numb fingers. Because his nose and cheeks were getting frostbitten, he pulled his scarf up over his face.

He no longer had any idea where he was—nothing looked familiar. Dimly he saw a slight downhill slope ahead. Surely it was too soon for it to be the one passing by the bombed-out farm. But maybe, with luck, it was the hill only two and a half kilometers from home.

Suddenly Berta lost her footing and fell, throwing the sleigh. They skidded and bounced downhill, then crashed into trees. Dāvids was thrown out and the load of loosened snow on the trees buried him.

Quickly he fought his way out, digging snow from under his scarf. The sleigh, snow-buried, was overturned and leaned at a drunken angle against some trees. The horse thrashed about weakly, tangled in the reins, and the big wooden harness that went up over her neck had snapped, the splintered wood piercing her neck. Blood stained the snow. That particular injury didn't look too severe, but Dāvids could see Berta's leg was broken.

There was nothing he could do for the horse. He didn't have a gun to put her out of her misery, and she was much too heavy for him to move. Shivering uncontrollably, he felt only despair. He couldn't make it home on foot—not in these drifts—especially when he was no longer sure exactly where he was. The snow covered anything that might have been familiar.

The sleigh was tipped so that the bed of it could be used to shield him from the vicious wind. Digging frantically with gloved hands, he scooped out the loose snow that had tumbled onto it, until there was a cave-like shelter. Quickly he sat in it, facing out, wrapped in his blanket, while he shivered.

He stared out at the bleak scene before him — a vast white emptiness with the one red-stained spot fast being covered by the blowing snow. Berta was no longer thrashing, and he didn't know if she had frozen to death yet or not.

He wondered how long it would be before he himself froze.

CHAPTER 11

DARKNESS CLOSED in, and still the wind blew, and every so often a limb cracked like a pistol shot as the weight of snow became too heavy. Dāvids continued to stare at the white scene before him as he shivered uncontrollably. He was probably close to home—but he might as well have been in Siberia—so unfamiliar was the landscape.

Remembering Siberia brought thoughts of Papus. For years he had assumed Papus was dead, since they had never received any word from him, but he couldn't help but wonder if somewhere out there—in a place as desolate as this—Papus was struggling to survive against the same kind of bitter cold. Was he still alive, saddened by the awareness of his son's betrayal?

A misery, such as Dāvids had not known in a long time, engulfed him. Believing Papus was dead had given him a blunted sort of inner peace. At least Papus no longer suffered.But thinking of him as maybe being alive brought back the guilt that turned in him like razor-sharp knives.

Had he sent Papus to a living death—Papus, whose only crime was helping a Jew?

He thought of Jēkabs sitting in that cave during a winter, looking out over a bleak peat bog. Poor miserable man, how did he stand it? No doubt Papus had gotten food to him somehow, but even food couldn't make a cold, lonely cave tolerable. Yet Jēkabs *had* survived. Dāvids marveled at the power of the human will to carry on.

He lowered his head to his knees, once again writhing under the load of guilt. He saw the prisoners that he worked with—those miserable, cold, suffering scraps of humanity—hungry for food, but hungrier more for a sign of compassion, a sign that someone regarded them as something more than despised animals. No matter that maybe they had once treated others the same way. Papus would not have worked among them without feeling. Papus, who helped a lonely Jew, would have helped a lonely Russian, too.

Again Dāvids felt the unworthiness. He could never be the man his father had been. He saw the pointing finger of his nightmares. It seemed to say, "This one is not my son. This one is concerned only with his personal resentments, his hates. This one should be dead."

The thought of death stayed with Dāvids. Total blackness engulfed the night. His shivering stopped and he grew drowsy. That was a sign he was freezing to death—and he was glad. He didn't deserve to live, to go home to Papus's farm. In his numbed thinking, it seemed right—that if he died, somehow Papus would live. Papus would come back to reclaim his farm.

Two limbs cracked simultaneously, then in about thirty seconds another snapped, followed by a different sound. From somewhere in Dāvids's stupor came the realization that what he'd heard was not breaking limbs —but a gun. And the other sound was a voice calling!

Somehow he managed to rouse himself enough to yell, "Hello-o-o."

Again came the voice whipped by the wind. Dāvids wanted to die, yet some instinct of self-preservation made him call out again. Suddenly a flashlight beam pierced the darkness, swept over the area and swung around till it zeroed in on his face. Someone leading a horse came over to him. It was Peter!

"Are you hurt?" Peter asked as the light swept quickly over Dāvids and the overturned sleigh.

Dāvids shook his head as the shivering began again. His mind didn't seem to function. "W-where'd you get a gun?" was all he could think to say.

"I've always had it—kept it hidden," was the reply. Peter shoved a chunk of rye bread at him. "Eat this, it'll help your body produce heat. I'll be right back."

He walked away and Dāvids looked at the bread but didn't eat it. He felt nothing—just an immense emptiness, as though he was already dead. In a short while Peter returned and dumped a bundle beside him. Taking a small shovel from the bundle, he dug the cave deeper, piling up the loose snow in front to make a nest-like shelter. Next he took a blanket from the bundle and draped it over the sleigh so it shielded the shelter even more from the wind. Then he crawled inside. "I put a blanket over Melnis—tied him among the trees—out of the wind. He'll be all right."

The rest of the bundle consisted of two blankets Māmiņa had made a long time ago by stitching sheepskins together. These were often used when going sleigh-riding because they were so warm. Peter wrapped one around Dāvids, and one around himself.

"Eat your bread," he ordered when he noticed Dāvids still holding it. But Dāvids didn't move. Peter turned off the flashlight and pulled Dāvids close to his big body.

Dāvids stiffened. "No—let me die!" he cried out.

Peter didn't release him, and despite Dāvids's wish to die, the warmth and closeness of another body was so comforting that he didn't have the will power to pull away.

"I don't deserve to live," he mumbled into the blanket.

Peter didn't ask questions—just held him until he stopped shivering. He was strong—like Papus—and Dāvids ached with longing for his father. Papus had often held him like this when he was little and upset or scared of something. Now he wanted Papus to hold him, to say he was forgiven.

"I betrayed Papus," he sobbed. "They took him—I—I told them about the radio—now he's dead—or in a place like this—because of me."

Peter murmured something in Russian, but Dāvids didn't understand.

"And Jēkabs—" Dāvids continued, needing to bare his tortured soul. "He was a kind man. But he's dead—because of me. Papus hid him from the Russians. Jēkabs asked me to—he hinted at it—"

"Hinted?" Peter asked softly.

"Why else would he tell me Papus hid him if it wasn't because he wanted *me* to hide him, too—from the Germans?"

"Maybe he just wanted you to know how kind your father had been."

"No—I killed him." Dāvids buried his face in Peter's

shoulder, glad it was pitch dark. "He was a lonely man. Somewhere he had a son—he told Valdis—but as far as anyone knew, in Latvia he had no one. But we loved him." Peter made a murmuring, understanding sound, but otherwise he said nothing. "I didn't like all Jews," Dāvids confessed. "Some of them were double-crossing—like anyone else—some betrayed our people. The Bolsheviks—they let some wealthy Jews live if they became traitors. There was one heading a prison in Jelgava—he was as brutal as any Bolshevik—tortured his own kind—and Latvians—but Jēkabs—" The lump in his throat made him swallow hard. "He couldn't be mean. He—he loved kids." Again his guilt and misery choked him. "But in the end a kid who could've helped him didn't."

Suddenly he jerked upright, unable to stand his own guilt, and lashed out at Peter. "Why did you have to come find me? Why didn't you mind your own business and let me die?"

"Would it bring Jēkabs or your father back?" came the quiet voice out of the blackness.

"No—but it's hell—remembering every single day what I did."

"I doubt anything you said was incriminating. Whatever reason they got him for—it's not important now. But it was not your fault." His voice became lower. "As for Jēkabs—hinting to be hidden would have endangered you—a child at the time—something he would never do. He probably knew his time was short—with the Nazis in control—and he couldn't die without letting someone in the family know how kind Jānis Ozols had been to him."

Peter's words acted like a balm on Dāvids's sorely crushing guilt. He felt it dissolve ever so slightly. But right on the heels of the release came a flood of shame. He was fifteen years old—almost sixteen—he'd proven himself a man capable of running a farm with Peter—of taking his punishment in the prison camp without breaking—and suddenly he had been crying on Peter's shoulder, like Kārlis might do, baring his innermost disgrace, telling the terrible secrets he'd never told anyone before.

To cover his shame, he turned angrily to Peter. "You never knew Jēkabs. How can you tell me what he would do? How could you—a Russian—know how a kindly Jewish man would feel?"

There was a long silence, then very softly Peter said, "*I'm his son.*"

How long it was before Dāvids spoke, he couldn't remember. It was unbelievable—Peter Krekov—a Jew! But it explained many things. Peter was often seen in Jēkabs's store. Peter had worked for Papus while Jēkabs had hidden in the cave—and surely Papus had known their relationship. It was probably Peter who had taken food to his own father, food given to him by Papus. And when Peter heard Papus had been deported, he braved certain danger to return to the farm, to help the family who had protected his father. It explained Peter's unfailing loyalty. Dāvids remembered also the day he tearfully told Peter that Jēkabs had been shot. There had been a long silence. No doubt it was Peter's first news of his father's death. And this would account for the expressionless face and the flat, lifeless voice when he said not to mourn the dead, but to work for the living. Now Dāvids understood why Peter never left the farm—even when Māmiņa asked him several times to go to Glūda or Auce or Bēne to get supplies. He'd always declined—saying it wasn't safe for a Russian to wander around. Yet tonight, to find the son of Jānis Ozols, he had set out, to go clear to Glūda if necessary, facing a blizzard, and firing a gun to attract attention. To possess a gun in Latvia — especially for a Russian — was punishable by death. Yet he had risked that.

Dāvids lay back against him, deeply moved. "I'm glad, Peter, I'm truly glad," he murmured. Peter's arm didn't tighten especially, but it was as though his love wrapped around Dāvids, warming him. Soon they both slept.

At dawn they climbed out of their snowbound cocoon and neither mentioned the conversation in the dark. The blizzard had ended, and mountainous piles of soft white snow blanketed everything. The sleigh was righted and though one side was badly damaged, the runners were still intact. Peter removed the broken harness from the stiff carcass of Berta, and by tying the break with the leather reins he'd used on Melnis, he was able to make it usable. Melnis, who had survived the storm, was put in harness and they headed home under a gray overcast sky.

Dāvids cast a sidelong glance at the big silent man beside him. Why had Peter told him his secret? To name himself a Jew was like signing his own death warrant. Then the answer came — in Peter's strange way he was saying that Dāvids's tearful confession of guilt would be regarded as a secret — as sacred to him as the one he himself had revealed.

As the days on the farm went by — days of singing and laughter and love and warmth of family — days full of delicious food — Dāvids's guilt subsided. Maybe, like Peter said, he hadn't given out any incriminating evidence. And the more he thought about it, the more he was sure of it, though he still could not remember everything he'd said or what was asked.

But he remembered clearly that he had confessed to

Papus that he had weakened under torture. No matter that it had been about something as inconsequential as owning a little radio. Papus had thought him guilty of betrayal and had refused to look at him. Dāvids knew that the only thing that would ever bring him total peace was the chance to explain to Papus himself what had happened in the NKVD office. But the chance to explain was gone forever, and Dāvids had to live with his memory.

During Dāvids's ten months in the camp, he'd heard only snatches of war news—mostly from new prisoners. They'd said the war was going badly for the Germans. But he'd discounted much of that because naturally a Russian would say his own army was winning. But at home he learned the truth—the German army had indeed suffered terrible losses in the Stalingrad fighting—losing over half a million men, and the new offenses in the Caucasus weren't going well, either.

Valdis stated that the German front, once almost seven hundred kilometers away from Latvia at the outskirts of Moscow to the north and as far east as Stalingrad to the south, was now pushed back. The northern divisions were not more than two or three hundred kilometers from the Latvian border. The news tended to add a somber note to the Christmas celebrations.

Almost every moment Dāvids was home, Māmiņa was with him, as though she wanted to crowd into a few days enough of him to carry her till the summer, when he would be home again. She smiled a lot and appeared happy, but to Dāvids she seemed more detached than ever. He had seen it in many of the prisoners. The doctors referred to it as "a departure from reality."

Valdis talked animatedly of the underground work being done along the war front, of railroads being blown up, of troop trains being derailed, of war-related factories being sabotaged. "The underground is really effective at the front," he said.

Kārlis was nervous, and quiet most of the time. Only in his drawings did the imaginative child come out. Though he saw the horrors of war around him, he preferred to draw pictures that were light, spontaneous, living.

One night after the family had retired, the boys sat on their beds facing one another. Kārlis prattled on, telling about the new worker Oskars had found to replace Gunārs—a fair-haired man named Arvīds.

"How're things going here on the farm?" Dāvids asked. "Any problems?"

Kārlis looked away. "I've tried keeping the inventory—like you did."

"Good—do we have a lot?"

The blond head bobbed, even as Kārlis shrugged. "Yes—sort of."

"Sort of?"

"Not much vodka."

Dāvids felt his chest constrict. "Oh?"

Kārlis looked at him with serious eyes. "Some cases were missing in June. I figured I'd counted wrong somehow, so I didn't worry too much about it. Then in November more cases gone—lots of it."

"Do you have any idea who took it?"

Again Kārlis averted his eyes. "I know you trust him—but I think it's Peter. I always did feel he was a spy."

Dāvids's shoulders sagged. He had been so sure that the stealing would stop with Gunārs gone. "Did you see Peter take it?"

"No."

"Did you find it in his cabin?"

"No."

"Then, why do you say Peter took it?"

Kārlis shrugged. "Just a feeling."

"What about this new guy—Arvīds? What do you know about him?"

"Not much. He's too simple-minded to be able to pull a stunt like hauling off ten cases of vodka at a time. In fact, I doubt that he even knows we have the stuff. Peter keeps him out of the grainery most of the time."

Dāvids began slowly to undress, his mind rebelling at the thought that Peter would steal from them. He was too wise a man to do something so obvious.

"Kārli, I can't believe it of Peter."

Kārlis lay back on his bed. "No, I didn't think you would." He rolled over on one elbow. "Then explain this—just before I discovered the missing cases, I saw Peter ride out one night on Melnis. It was late—at a time I'd normally be asleep. Frankly, I think he's a spy— delivering the stuff to Russian guerrillas."

Dāvids's sleep that night was not a peaceful one. He remembered the warm body next to his out in the blizzard, the gentle voice of understanding, the fact that Peter had risked much in coming to find him. Peter was loyal to them. He wanted to believe that. But another part of him said that his brother's suspicions were not the imaginations of a little boy. They struck awfully close to home.

Despite the discouraging war news or the mental deterioration in Māmiņa, Dāvids's holiday was a happy one. The farm had done as well as could be expected and the quotas had been met. Except for the ten missing cases, the larder was full. Coffee was nonexistent and tea was hard to get, as was white flour, but Marta had saved some of her meager stock to make sweet breads.

Though Dāvids spent a lot of time with Peter, as he was shown around the farm, there was a strained feeling between them. It distressed him, but he couldn't bring himself to question Peter about the losses.

"If it *is* Peter," he told Kārlis, "and all he takes from us is some vodka, then so be it. He has served us loyally. I can't accuse him. He's my friend, Kārli."

And so came the time to leave, and Dāvids solemnly shook Peter's hand. "Thanks, Peter—for everything," he said.

"Hurry back," was Peter's blunt reply.

Once back at the prison camp, Dāvids plunged into the familiar routine, seeing the same miserable faces every day—and a few new ones. In the evening the men in his building huddled around the one wood stove as though maybe its warmth would drive out some of their misery. Dāvids watched them, and in his mind came the memory of his night in the blizzard. On an impulse he walked to the kitchen. No one was around, and he stuffed into his shirt some bread and cheese. From now on he would do as he knew Papus would have done if he had been here. He entered the room and walked over toward the stove, hearing them speak in Russian. He had to fight the automatic resistance that crowded out his sudden impulse to help them.

Then one man turned around. Dāvids had not seen him here before. He was thin and jaundiced, and he bore scars of beating and torture. In fact, there was a black patch over one eye—probably the eye had been gouged out, Dāvids figured. Despite all of this, it was a face he knew he could never forget. It was the same face he saw in his nightmares. Skinny now, one-eyed, old—it made no difference.

"Comrade Shimkevich!" he said in a voice filled with loathing.

CHAPTER 12

"YOU KNOW ME?" the man asked in surprise.

Dāvids knew, then, that the NKVD man did not remember him. After all, he'd been a mere child then—he was a man now, taller, more muscular, and much changed. "No. I merely was told you were here—a new prisoner," he said coldly, clutching his coat about him to hide the food under his shirt. No way could he give anything to this beast—certainly not compassion.

Shimkevich seemed to accept his unfriendly reply and turned his attention back to the warm stove.

Dāvids walked away, seeing the other tired faces, and Māmiņa's words came back. "But we're Latvians—and Christians." He knew, deep in his heart, that Papus would feed even this man. He was harmless—a man who was now receiving the kind of savage brutality he had given.

It was a fierce battle inside him, the desire to spit at this man, to walk off and never come near any of them again. He could feel the muscles in his jaw knot. His stomach tightened, and his hate welled up till he felt almost ill. But finally he turned and walked back, handing the food to the men. Some of them thanked him.

That night he was sure that after seeing Comrade Shimkevich face to face he would have nightmares. But he slept soundly. Then again the next day he brought shriveled apples that he'd found in the bottom of a barrel and a small amount of sausage. Each day he added some little thing to their meager diet.

A lean, fair-haired German soldier named Friedrich, who was in charge of kitchen supplies, noticed him searching for food scraps and threatened to report him to the prison authorities. But Dāvids persisted in finding food for his miserable prisoners, and soon he realized Friedrich was deliberately leaving scraps around for him to take. As the days went by, Dāvids formed a quiet friendship with the soldier.

"You have a soul," Friedrich said softly, and Dāvids was sure that this man, drilled by the Nazi regime to be a ruthless soldier, nevertheless longed for goodness in his life. Friedrich was his only break from the horror of the tortured prisoners, and sometimes when he could not take the moaning and groaning any longer, he would seek out the soldier, and they would talk of other days. He learned that Friedrich was the son of a bookbinder in Cologne, Germany, that he hoped someday to be an architect. Unlike the other Germans in the prison camp, the military was not his life. He was a family-type man, talking often of his wife and three children, of his parents, and even of his grandparents.

As much as possible, Dāvids avoided Comrade Shimkevich. For one thing, the man's rabid desire for revenge made him perpetually ugly of disposition.

"That Vladimirov—he's responsible," he snarled one night. "I'll kill him if it's the last thing I ever do."

"Why?" another Russian officer asked. "Comrade Vladimirov is NKVD, like yourself. What have you got against him?"

Shimkevich picked up a hunk of firewood and threw it at the wall, as though envisioning Vladimirov sitting there. "A prisoner—I wanted him killed." Shimkevich growled, grinding his teeth in hate. "No—Vladimirov overrode my order—said, 'Send him to Siberia, then kill him.' But he got away—made a fool of me. I'll never forget that—never!" He spit on the floor. "It was the work of the underground—I'm sure of that." His one eye flickered over the others. "Did Vladimirov let me know about the escape in time? No—he went into hiding—and left me to bear the brunt. But I'll get him. Every torture I've suffered—he'll get it double. So will the prisoner—if I ever find him. But it's Vladimirov I want most. Because of him I got arrested by my own NKVD—and when the Gestapo took over the jail, I couldn't get away." He spewed out a torrent of profanity, cursing Vladimirov for having him jailed so he could not flee when the Germans overran Jelgava.

One day, following the usual bad news of the German defeats that infiltrated into the prison, Friedrich came to his small room and sat on the edge of his cot. No one else was around.

"Germany is losing the war, Dāvid," he said with deep sadness. "It's hard to swallow. Hitler promised us victory."

"Maybe there'll be a reversal, and the Russians will be driven back," Dāvids said, wanting to lift his friend's spirits. Friedrich looked so utterly defeated.

"No. The Bolsheviks will return to your country," Friedrich said flatly. He looked around, and seeing no one in the room, he said in a low voice, "Get out while you can, my friend."

"Out? You mean out of Latvia!" Everything in Dāvids rebelled at the thought. "Where would we go?"

"Anywhere. Go to Germany. But try to reach the Allies. They're your only hope."

Dāvids remembered how the British had helped them achieve their freedom in 1918 and hope flared in his heart. Surely the British—and maybe the Americans—would not let them be swallowed by the Russians. True, right now the British were having troubles of their own, fighting Hitler's army. But Dāvids had no doubt they would eventually be victorious, then Latvia would be free. His sense of dejection lifted, and with more cheer than he'd felt in a long time he got some scraps and carried them out to his miserable prisoners.

As always, when they huddled around the one stove in the great hall before being locked in their cells for the night, their talk was of the revenge they so passionately craved. Occasionally they varied this pattern by talking of elaborate escapes. Sometimes it would be one they'd heard of, or even taken part in, or how they would get out of this prison. Dāvids knew the latter discussions were impossible—complex plans that they made up for their own amusement, and for that reason they discussed them in his presence. But he knew secret plans floated around, because occasionally an escape attempt would be made.

"I'll get out of here yet," Comrade Shemkevich said one evening when the others talked of previous escapes. "And when I do, I'll find that Vladimirov." His one eye narrowed, and his face with its ghastly hue looked mean.

"Yeah, we've all got enemies we want to wipe out," a young prisoner named Yuri said without rancor. "Trouble is, we're here and they're out there —someplace—free."

"Well, one day I'll be out there," came Shimkevich's angry growl.

Dāvids shivered, remembering this man's total lack of feeling, while he himself had been beaten. Shimkevich fought to survive for one reason only—to torture those he blamed for his predicament.

A week later Dāvids heard he was caught trying to dig his way out of the compound. He knew the condition in which the miserable man would be returned to the cell—battered, bloody, moaning in pain, and near death. The Gestapo were masters at halting the torture at the point where the victim would suffer agonies but would not die. That was why he, Dāvids, was there—to feed them and keep them alive so they could be tortured again.

It wasn't sympathy for Comrade Shimkevich but compassion to another human being that made him smuggle out a bottle of aspirin. Such weak medicine wasn't much in the face of so much pain, but it was the best he could do.

"Why are you kind to us?" a one-handed man named Andrei asked him after seeing him give Comrade Shimkevich the medicine.

"Because I hope somewhere in Siberia—if my father is alive—that someone is doing as much for him," Dāvids replied softly and walked away.

His reply, however, seemed to have touched a few of his prisoners, and as the days went by, they seemed to become his friends.

His sixteenth birthday came and passed, and as often as possible Dāvids brought comfort to his charges. After he'd been doing this for over a month, it occurred to him that he no longer had the lonely deserted feeling he'd had the previous year. Some of these men were now his friends, especially Andrei, and Yuri, who bore scars on his back from beatings. They were not NKVD men, but farmers who had been drafted into the Red army and had been captured in the assault on Stalingrad. Dāvids and the two men often sat huddled around the stove, discussing crops, seeds, and dairy cattle, and he shared with them the pictures Kārlis had sketched. When he saw tears of homesickness in their eyes, he felt close to them. They were soldiers because, like him, they were forced to obey. But at heart they were farmers—lonely for the smell of freshly turned earth, of manure, of fresh milk.

When Dāvids had first begun to mix with the men, the authorities had protested, and several times they beat him, but finally they said no more when it became apparent that there was less disciplinary problems with his group than any other. Also, he suspected that Friedrich intervened on his behalf. So Dāvids moved more or less freely now.

Finally came the summer day when he was called again to the office and told to pack his clothes. His fifteen months of service were ended. He was given a ticket home.

After packing his few belongings, he went to visit his charges as they sat eating their meager lunch.

"I'm going home," he said and sat at the end of the table feeling as though he was deserting friends.

There was a generally noisy reaction to his news— some wishing him the best of luck, others making ribald jokes.

"Oh, God," Yuri groaned, "what I'd give to be able to say those three words!"

"Maybe someday you will, Yuri. A war doesn't go on forever," Dāvids reminded him.

"Just to get out of here—that's all I ask," Comrade Shimkevich muttered.

"It'd take a bomb to get anyone out of here," Yuri said bitterly.

"Speaking of bombs and escapes," Andrei spoke up, "I remember one—it was near Moscow. I was on a troop train—heading to the front." He paused to explain. "This was way back when the Germans were about to take Latvia from us."

"Go on, go on," one man said impatiently, as the group frequently did when someone told a story. "What about the escape?"

Andrei chuckled. "Anyway, we stopped at this little town on a very dark night—and another train, heading to Siberia and loaded with prisoners, pulled in. Suddenly a bomb went off." He waved his one hand. "Loudest bang you ever heard—ripped off a door. Guess it was more smoke than anything, to cause confusion."

"Did it?" Dāvids asked when Andrei paused for effect.

"Seven men got away," Andrei replied with a knowing nod. "They caught some of them. I remember one man—saw him clearly in the light from the depot. Had a scar—like a white streak across the side of his head—not a very big—"

"That's the one!" Comrade Shimkevich roared, his scarred face contorted in anger. "Jānis Ozols—that's the man I want to get. He was one of the prisoners they never found. That escape—it was the work of the underground—I know it was—I *know* it!" His face was livid, so the scars stood out in ghastly jagged lines. "I wanted him killed in Jelgava." A sob tore out of his throat and his bony shoulders sagged in his own personal misery. "But no—Comrade Valdimirov, my superior—he insisted we rush him out of Latvia." He slumped back into his chair—a broken man consumed with hate. "I'd worked a long, long time to get Ozols. He had outwitted me time and time again. We could've gotten him a lot earlier, but we wanted to find his hiding cache. It was my great achievement—getting him at last and putting an end to the smuggling of arms to the underground. And he was my downfall." A cruel smile distorted his face. "He probably never made it out of Russia. That scar made him too easily spotted. Even if he did, he'd end up in the hands of the Nazis." He touched his battered face and grimaced. "And we all know the Gestapo is no saint, either."

The men noisily agreed, repeating timeworn tales of Nazi brutality, but Dāvids sat unheeding. He rose as in a fog and bid the men farewell. His glance lingered on Comrade Shimkevich's cruel, ugly face. He felt no hate—just a kind of numb satisfaction. This man was behind bars—consumed with hate. And maybe—just maybe—Papus was alive and free. It seemed right to him.

He searched for Friedrich, his one German friend among these coldhearted Nazi guards, to bid him good-bye, and he found him out in the courtyard. The blond man clasped his hand warmly. "I'm glad you're going back to your family, Dāvid. I wish I could do the same." He lowered his voice. "But remember what I say—get out while you can. Get to England—or America."

Dāvids nodded, but he had no intention of leaving his beloved farm. No, he would remain, and England or America would help the Latvians rid their country of the cruel yoke of the Red army.

By the time Dāvids arrived in Glūda, he learned that the war situation was desperate. The Red army had just about driven the Nazis out of the Soviet Union altogether; there was talk of the Nazis fleeing Latvia and leaving it to the Russians again, and everything was chaotic. Though he had heard this from Friedrich, he hadn't realized it was so bad. The distressing news almost wiped out his elation that Papus might be alive somewhere.

He decided to walk home, to give himself time to think, to adjust to the new events, and to savor the familiar sights. His possessions hung from a knapsack on his back, and he walked along in his bare feet, hands deep in his pockets, as the gentle breeze ruffled his untidy brown hair. His pants were too short and his shirt stretched across his shoulders, showing he had grown in the past year.

In Glūda he heard much talk about Latvians fleeing their country. Many had tried going to Sweden, but the German and Russian navies sank or arrested the fishing vessels jammed with refugees. Also, there was a shortage of gasoline, making it almost impossible to sail the 150 miles to Swedish shores. So they streamed to Germany. It was the only place for them to go—to escape the Soviets, whom they feared more than the Nazis. Dāvids, like many farmers, resisted the impulse to flee to the western front. This was his beloved land.

He turned the bend at the north end by the bombed-out farm, which was now being managed by a Latvian family. Then his own farm came into view—how beautiful it was! Despite the troubles and the shortage of good help, it was in pretty fair repair, and the newly plowed fields were green with tiny oat and barley seedlings. He grinned—Peter evidently had no notion of running away. And neither did he. Making this decision, he walked with a more determined step and his jaw got the stubborn set.

As he neared, he saw Kārlis with the cows out in the pasture. He sat on a big rock, hunched over a sketch pad, so intent on his work that he did not see Dāvids.

"Hey, Kārli—I'm home!" came the triumphant yell. Immediately Kārlis dropped his pad and came charging across the field, finally slamming into Dāvids in an exuberant embrace.

After a joyous noisy welcome, the two brothers walked down the lane. Kārlis had grown too, and at age ten, he was only about ten centimeters shorter than Dāvids, though he still retained the round-faced childish appearance.

Dāvid, what're we going to do?" he asked, jumping up and down in nervous excitement. "Are we going to leave? Māmiņa wants to. She's scared of the Bolshies. Will we have to give up the farm? If we do, where will we live? What'll we do?"

"I don't know yet," Dāvids said irritably to stem the tide of questions. "Give me time to find out what's going on." Then, half teasing, he asked, "Has there been any more vodka missing?"

Kārlis didn't laugh. "Yes—about the end of February. It was snowing when I went to bed. Then during the night it stopped. The next morning I saw footprints leading from the grainery. I checked and saw five cases missing." He turned the wide, serious eyes to Dāvids. "Want to know where they led?"

Dāvids felt a stab of fear. He didn't want to say it. "To Peter's cabin?"

"Right. And you know what else? I saw hoofprints in the snow—leading to the woods. He's a spy, I tell you."

Dāvids laughed to hide his consternation. "You've got your secret agents mixed, little brother. Why would a spy steal vodka? Spies work with the underground and get military secrets and blow up bridges, and things like that. All Peter does is work like a horse on this farm."

"Then explain the missing vodka," Kārlis challenged.

"Maybe he's hiding another—" He checked himself just in time. He'd almost said another Jew. "Maybe he's got—he's got a friend somewhere who likes vodka," he ended lamely.

No more was said and they hurried to the house. Dāvids's welcome home was as though he was a returning war hero, and once again Marta cooked his favorite foods, and as he slathered the sweet butter on his bread, he thought of Yuri and Andrei, and he felt a twinge of sadness. If only he could give them a crock of butter and some of the roast pork that permeated the house with such a delicious smell. How their haggard faces would light up! And when he saw all the family around the table, he wished Friedrich could be here. How happy it would make him!

Peter's welcome, like everything about the man, was reserved. And Dāvids, when he extended his hand, wanted to sound glad to see him, but Kārlis's accusation kept drumming in his mind. Consequently his welcome to Peter was equally as reserved.

That night, weary from the excitement of home-coming, he went to bed early. He could hear Kārlis breathing deeply, but sleep for himself would not come. His thoughts went from Papus to Peter, Peter to Papus, so that his emotions danced between joy, suspicion, and heartache. He did not want to doubt Peter. He had been consistently loyal to them. After what Papus had done—sheltering Jēkabs and letting Peter work here to be near his father—Peter simply could not betray them. If Peter was stealing the vodka—and the evidence *did* point to him—he had to have an urgent need for it.

Then his own words came back—"spies work for the underground." And who else had mentioned underground? Then he remembered. Comrade Shimkevich had said the underground had freed Papus.

Dāvids sat bolt upright in bed. Peter—Papus! That had to be the answer. Silently, yet frantically, he threw on his clothes and tiptoed down the steps and out of the house. Racing to the cabin, he banged on the door.

"Who is it?" came Peter's sleep-fogged voice.

"Me. I want to talk to you."

"Can't it wait till morning?"

"No."

In a moment the door opened, and Peter, clad only in shorts, let him in. After shutting the door and pulling the blackout curtains across the open window, he turned on a light. Then he looked wearily at Dāvids, though he said nothing.

"Is my father alive?" Dāvids asked.

The weary, bored look slowly gave way, and Peter's face became expressionless. He pulled on his pants that were hanging over a chair, then he reached for a shirt. "How should I know?" he asked casually.

"Because you're stealing vodka to deliver to the underground. I think you know about Papus."

Peter gave a half smile as he searched in the cupboard for a plate of cookies. "I could be selling it to Russian friends," he said and extended the plate. "Here, have some."

Dāvids ignored the plate. "I don't think you would. It's not like you. You've been loyal to us—you would be loyal to Papus—because of Jēkabs. You'd have to have a very good reason to steal from us. I think the reason is Papus."

Peter chuckled as he put the untouched plate on the

table and sat down. "Dāvid, you sound like Kārlis. He thinks I'm a spy and—"

Dāvids planted himself spraddle-legged in front of him. "Quit fussing around like an old lady. It's not like you," he raged. "Forget the cookies." He yanked Peter's arm, forcing him to look up at him. "You're evading the issue. I heard Papus escaped—an explosion on a train—and about every four to six months since then you've snitched some vodka—our most profitable item. Five cases of first-grade vodka will bring a good price. I think you're sending it—or the money for it—to my father." He held Peter's eyes. "Are you?" he growled.

"Sit down," Peter said and rose to close the window, even though no one lived in the cabin next to him. Then he sat down. The single overhead bulb made strong shadows on his bony face, and his dark eyes were hidden in the blackness of the deep-set sockets. "Keep your voice down," he growled, then added, "How'd you learn?"

"Comrade Shimkevich—he's a prisoner," Dāvids said softly. "There was talk about various escapes. He mentioned Jānis Ozols. He was furious because Papus got away."

Peter's face creased in a slow, vengeful smile. "So—our Comrade is now getting what he dished out." He sounded pleased.

"Papus—tell me about him."

"I arranged the explosion. I knew Comrade Vladimirov—the head of NKVD in Jelgava. We were schoolmates in Russia." He gave a bitter smile. "He never knew I am part Jew, of course. We would hardly have been friends." The smile vanished. "I arranged a dinner when your father was taken. He told me they had gotten a confession and they would kill Ozols for his crime. I said I'd heard the underground was very strong in this part of the country, and he'd be smarter to ship Ozols to Russia—*then* kill him. He did."

"And you arranged the bombing so Papus could get away," Dāvids said in awe.

"Yes."

"Where is he?"

"I don't know. He went first to my sister in Smolensk. She smuggled him to our uncle in the Ukraine."

"And the vodka?"

"Financed his moves. It now finances the underground there—to help others to get out of Russia."

A feeling of pride flowed through Dāvids. His vodka had helped free Papus from the Bolsheviks, and it was helping to free others. He grinned. "And now?"

"Now I wait till the underground contacts me again—if they can."

"At the cave?"

Peter looked surprised. "So you *did* find the cave! I often wondered." Then he shook his head. "At first, yes—but then I dug a new cave—just beyond the bog. I wasn't sure how much you knew."

Dāvids remembered Peter's questioning the first time he'd gone to get peat.

"Can't Papus come home? What was his crime?" he asked.

Peter toyed idly with the cookie plate. "For many months he smuggled guns to the underground—hid them in the cave—"

Dāvids gasped. Papus had done exactly what *he* had done! Evidently Valdis and Daila had not known about the smuggling then, the hiding of Jēkabs, or the existence of the cave. Valdis's only part in the underground at that time had probably been that of a soldier in hiding. Dāvids felt proud, knowing Papus's family was carrying on his work.

"The Soviets have guerrilla spies," Peter continued, "here in Latvia. If your father was discovered—he'd be dead in a week." He brushed his hand across his black hair as though indicating Papus's scar. "He is easily identified."

"Can I tell Māmiņa?" Dāvids asked. "It'd help her—"

"*No!*" Peter said emphatically. "Absolutely not. In Latvia only you and I *know* he is alive. Let it be so."

Dāvids nodded and they sat in silence. After a while Dāvids flushed guiltily. "Peter, I've almost hated you sometimes—specially since Christmas—knowing you were stealing our vodka."

Peter glanced up suddenly—an expression on his face that Dāvids could not define. "So *that's* why you avoided me."

"Why did you think I did?"

"Because you'd learned I am part Jewish."

"*Peter!*"

"Thank you," Peter said softly. "I'm glad I was wrong." He extended his big callused hand and Dāvids grasped it tightly. He felt the same warmth flow from Peter to him that he'd felt the night in the blizzard.

Later, as he headed to the door, he paused. "Peter—who confessed about Papus?"

"I—I don't know," Peter replied, looking down to get a cookie from the plate.

"I think you do."

"Even if I did—what difference would it make now? The main thing is—your father is alive." Peter rose. "Good night."

When Dāvids returned to bed and lay there thinking of the conversation, it occurred to him that Peter was unaware that he, Dāvids, had also delivered guns. At least he'd made no mention of it. And Peter spoke of the underground helping Papus get out of Russia. Peter *knew* of the existence of the Latvian underground, but he probably knew little or nothing about it. But he *did* know of an underground unit working in Russia, and it was this one that had helped Papus.

Dāvids felt proud that even in his small way he'd been part of the underground work. Though their army was small, and the two separate units were of different nationalities—at least they had one aim—to free men from enslavement. And he knew that if the chances came again, he would willingly serve—regardless of the risk.

It was now the end of July, and one day in Glūda Dāvids saw German soldiers, most of them bloody and in tatters, streaming through town, on their way to the ports. They were deserting Latvia by the thousands as the Russian army drove them relentlessly westward. Could this be the same army that had paraded so victoriously through here exactly three years ago? Dāvids wondered in disbelief, proud men marching vigorously while the streets rumbled with heavy artillery? Now they shuffled, defeat written in every line of their tired bodies.

The side roads were choked with Latvian families fleeing the eastern provinces. They could not tolerate the thought of living under the heel of communism again. Time had only made the Soviets more aggressive, more brutal.

At home, Māmiņa was frantic to join the exodus.

"We can't go without Daila," Dāvids argued. His sister had so far resisted leaving, saying she couldn't go without Valdis, who was still at the front. "Besides, I can't leave my farm," he added. This was no longer true—but he used it to strengthen his argument. As dearly as he loved his land, he had another priority now—to find his father. But he had to have some idea where to look before starting out, and lived in the hope that somehow, soon, Peter would hear again from the underground, and perhaps they would give him some indication as to where Jānis Ozols had gone, if he had gotten out of the Soviet Union.

CHAPTER 13

IN SEPTEMBER the Germans made a strong counter-attack, and the Red army pulled back. The threat to Latvia seemed over, and the flood of refugees abated. And still no word came from the underground. Arvīds and Verners had fled, and Peter, Dāvids, and Kārlis did the best they could to harvest the crop. Frail Rolfs tended the cows in the pasture. But there was no *talka* — the man with the thresher was gone.

At Dāvids's request, Daila had a forged passport made for Peter. He was listed as Peteris Ozols — their half brother — and if they were forced to flee, he would travel with them. At first Peter had resisted, saying it might endanger the family if it was ever discovered that he was actually a Russian — and half Jewish also. But when Dāvids reminded him that they needed him to help them if they had to escape, and also to help find Papus, Peter finally consented.

In October Valdis came home, and he and Daila left

their little house in Glūda and moved to the farm. He said he was not returning to the front.

"Did they let all the Latvians go?" Dāvids asked in surprise when he saw his pale, thin brother-in-law. The rigors of war had left their mark on Valdis, though he had not been injured. But his eyes were haunted by what he'd seen and done.

Valdis pulled out an important-looking paper. Dāvids recognized it immediately—a certificate proving ownership of a horse. Many years before, the Latvian government, in order to cut down on horse stealing, made it mandatory that a certificate be issued each time a horse was sold. It was a large, official-looking paper with all sorts of stamps and signatures. Dāvids craned his neck and read the name—Berta. This was the certificate for the gray mare that died in the blizzard!

"I used this," Valdis boasted with a smile.

"How?" Kārlis asked.

"A lot of Germans can't read Latvian," he said with a laugh. "But they're not about to admit it. Well, we had a guard at our post—a rather slow-witted lout, too proud to admit he didn't know everything. So I showed this to him one night. He asked me why it was not in German, and I said, 'It's in Latvian because I'm Latvian. That's only natural,' and he believed me, the stupid fool. I said it was a special permit, allowing me to come home because my wife was gravely ill." He laughed again, pleased by his trickery. "So he let me go." He folded the paper and put it in his pocket. "And I don't plan to go back. The Bolsheviks will push the Germans back, and I'm not going to be fodder for the Nazis. I can't go underground because the Nazis would recognize me, so I'm getting out while I can "

The underground, according to Daila, were re-
trenching, mainly in the Kurzeme Province along the
Baltic coast. They knew they couldn't stem the Red tide,
and that Latvia would soon be under Communist rule
again. But they would constantly disrupt things in hopes
the British and Americans would intervene in their
behalf and force other countries to help liberate them.

"They say people like us," she explained, "those who
aren't trained guerrillas, should leave. Then when the
war is over, we'll be in a position to help the guerrillas
here, keeping them supplied. So we'd better get ready to
go."

Within days it was clear Valdis was right—the German
counterattack was over. It had been staged merely to give
the German officials time to get out of Latvia and take as
much as they could with them.

The following day Oskars arrived with his loaded
wagon. "Elita—Dāvid," he exclaimed, his hands twitch-
ing nervously. "We *must* leave. The brick factory—blown to bits—Nazis destroying everything they
can't take with them. Bridges—buildings—factories—everything gone! The Soviets are already in
Latgale Province! They're bombing. We must flee while
there's still a chance!"

The rest of the day was one of total chaos. They had
already sorted out the things they would take when they
left. Now everyone suddenly had other ideas. Treasures
they had set aside to leave behind became too precious.
Māmiņa wanted to take old heirloom furniture and
sobbed when Oskars said no.

"Pack the warmest clothes you have," he told her.
"Winter's coming."

"Don't forget the passports," Daila called out,
clutching to her breast a collection of old dolls she'd

gotten from the attic. But when Valdis shook his head, she set them lovingly on the sofa.

"Take food," Valdis kept saying over and over. "Take more food than anything."

"And vodka," Kārlis piped up. "It's like having money—better even."

Everyone bustled around, frantically chosing this and discarding that, only to throw out what they'd chosen. In the distance they could hear bombing.

Dāvids counted all the money they had—German occupation marks—satisfied that over the years they had accumulated a reasonable amount. He stuffed them in the lining of all the coats, in boots, rolled it in underwear, and put the largest notes in a money belt around his waist.

That night they could see the glow in the sky of fires in Jelgava. Latvia was really taking a beating. Not only were the retreating Germans blowing up most of the industries and rail centers, but the approaching Red army were bombing steadily. Their aim had improved. The front line was now only twenty or thirty kilometers away.

By dawn the next morning they were finally ready to leave. All the cows and horses that they weren't taking with them were turned loose. The three wagons were loaded with all the clothes, vodka, cigarettes, crocks of butter, ham, cheese, bacon, dried fruits, bread, flour, and honey they could carry. Food was scarce in the beleaguered cities, and with it they would buy their way to safety. Māmiņa rode in one wagon with Marta and Rolfs; Daila and Valdis traveled with Oskars, and Dāvids and Kārlis rode with Peter. Trailing behind each wagon was a spare horse and a cow.

With eyes misting over, Dāvids mounted his wagon. As they drove down the lane, he gave one last look at his beloved farm. He ached at leaving the comfortable old home, the big tree in the back yard, its leaves now turning yellow, the cows lowing out in the pasture, the grainery with its now-empty contraband pits. For three years it had belonged to him—but now it would belong to some Bolshevik family. He wished he could give it to Yuri or Andrei. They would take care of it.

Despite his melancholy, he had a feeling of excitement. This was the first step in his search for Papus. Somewhere—somehow—they would meet. His father would know they were forced to flee. And Germany was the only place they could go. Then Dāvids would be able to tell him that he had known nothing of the smuggled guns, that he had not weakened and betrayed him.

He gave one last glance at the farm. Everything familiar in his life, everything he had ever felt dear, was now a part of his past. And before him lay—what? Where once he had been the son of a well-to-do farmer, now he was part of the teeming mass of refugees, whose lot was danger and misery. But at the end, hopefully, was Papus.

Resolutely he turned his face forward, aware of Kārlis crying beside him.

The next few days were unending stretches of dust and roads clogged with other refugees, of rain and mud, of cold nights and miserable humid days, of tired horses and exhausted and irritable people, of the incessant thunder of bombs behind them, and fleeing German soldiers ahead of them, of interrupted meals and disturbed sleep, of the night skies red with fires. The woods all around them teemed with the vanguard of the Communist army, whose snipers created total panic. Few of the refugees had guns, since all firearms had been confiscated first by the Russians, and then by the Germans.

In Dāvids's group, Peter had his pistol, well hidden, and Valdis carried his army rifle buried under the wagon seat.

They traveled far into the night before halting on the side of the road in utter exhaustion. Sometimes, when Kārlis begged to ride with Māmiņa, Peter and Dāvids would talk quietly, speculating on the chances of finding Papus. Like Dāvids, Peter was confident that Jānis Ozols would search until he found his family. In the three years he had been gone, he had not dared return to Latvia. But surely he would go into Germany to find them.

Dāvids learned a little about Peter—that his non-Jewish mother had divorced his father when Peter was about fourteen and his sister twelve, that Peter had lived in Czechoslovakia with her for a while, then had returned to Russia to live with his father. When the Russians began the senseless slaughter of wealthy Jews, Jēkabs had fled to Latvia, and Peter had returned to Czechoslovakia, only to set out later and search in Latvia until he found his father. He had come as a Russian farmer and lived on various small farms within a day's or two day's ride from Glūda, so he could do his purchasing in the general store and see Jēkabs. When the Russians fled the country, Peter had been hurt staging the explosion near Moscow, and had slowly and painfully made his way back to the Ozols farm, keeping in the woods until he could hide in the hay.

Dāvids confided in Peter that he and Daila and Valdis had worked with the underground, smuggling guns like his father had done.

"You mean that girl—Daila—why she's just a child —you mean she worked with the underground!" Peter gasped.

"She's twenty-two, Peter—she's not a child," Dāvids reminded him, smiling.

Peter shook his head in amazement. "So like your father—both of you." There was clear admiration in his voice. And when he looked at Daila in the wagon ahead, there was a softness on his face. It occurred to Dāvids that Peter had a very tender feeling for the girl, something he'd always kept carefully hidden.

The first two days out, Māmiņa had done fine, driving her wagon, looking strong and determined. Getting out of Latvia seemed to be what she needed. But sniper fire killed the woman in the wagon ahead of her on the third day, and later in the afternoon a bomb fell on the road not too far ahead, blasting wagons and animals and people in all directions. The screams, the force of the explosion, the dust and flying debris, as well as the stench of blood, covered them like a blanket. A part of a wagon slammed into Peter, breaking his arm. Māmiņa screamed—not just one loud cry of fright, but a continuous piercing scream of a mind that could no longer accept the horrors inflicted on it. Oskars tossed the reins to Valdis and leaped on her wagon, cradling her in his arms, muffling the scream until she finally slumped against him, staring off into space, hiccuping as she tried to stifle her sobs. Once again she withdrew from the terrors around her.

Among the refugees they found a doctor who set Peter's arm and put it in a sling, and who gave Māmiņa a sedative to quiet her.

The next morning, when they were ready to leave, Dāvids tried to encourage her and she gave an empty smile. "Yes, dear," she murmured. Then she turned questioning blue eyes to him. "Dāvid—where's your father? Where's my Jānka?" The question startled him. Did she know Papus was alive, and that he and Peter were hoping to locate him? He hesitated. Peter said no one else should know, but he *had* to tell her. Maybe it would help her to return to reality if she had something to cling to. "Māmin—we're looking for Papus," he murmured, caressing her arm. "When we get to Germany, we'll find him."

"Why isn't he here, now?" she said peevishly. "Why isn't he here when I need him? Go get him, Dāvid, like a good boy. Tell him I'm tired of driving the wagon." When Dāvids didn't move, she pulled her arm away. "Go, do as you're told," she snapped. "Tell Jānis to get up here. I wish he wouldn't wander off and leave me to take care of everything. It's not like him."

"Yes, Māmin," Dāvids said, blinking back tears. The Jānis she was looking for was not the man somewhere in a far-off country but the husband of three years ago, the one who in her mind was still here in Latvia, somewhere nearby, who would come at her bidding and take over.

On the fourth night they saw a farmhouse near the road, and they were able to trade food and a cow for permission to sleep in their guest rooms. For the first time since leaving home they changed their clothes and bathed.

The closer they got to the port city of Liepaja, the more they began to see the total destruction of the "scorched earth" policy of the retreating Germans. Dāvids had heard of it when the Soviets retreated three years ago, but he wasn't prepared for what he saw. Bridges were blown up, in places roads were nothing more than bomb craters, trees were splintered like kindling, and towns were totally destroyed. A factory was now only gutted walls, twisted steel, broken windows, and rubble. Gangs of workers carried covered bodies to mass graves.

The straggling column of exhausted and numbed

refugees scattered at the first sound of planes, heading for the woods that bordered the roads in places. But even that afforded little protection, since the Russians also bombed and strafed the woods. That night they saw the flames of Liepaja lighting the sky, as wave after wave of planes went overhead.

"How'll we get through that?" Kārlis asked, his teeth chattering in fright. "How, Dāvid? We'll all be blown up. I want to go back to the farm. I'm scared. How're we going to get to Germany, anyhow? What'll we do with our wagons? Where—?"

"Kārli, shut up!" Dāvids roared at him. "I don't know how or what we'll do. All we—"

"Let's go back to the farm."

"There probably isn't a farm anymore," he said with a catch in his voice. He wondered if there was even the port city of Liepaja left. Papus had visited the city often, coming with Oskars, and he had many friends there. Dāvids had thought maybe he'd ask one of them to put them up for a day or two—till Māmiņa was calmer. But he didn't know where any of them lived. And anyway, Liepaja was no safer now than any other place in Latvia. No—they had to catch the first boat to Germany. In another day or so there wouldn't be any more Latvia as they knew it.

The next day was one Dāvids knew he would never forget. As they neared the outskirts of the city, the air was rank with the stench of dead bloated animals, exposed outhouses, ruptured sewers, and smoldering ruins. Hardly a building was standing. People scurried about, dazed and glassy-eyed. Ambulances screamed their way through streets, gathering the injured. Haggard-faced men carried wrapped bodies to waiting trucks.

"This way," Oskars yelled, waving his arm, and he led

them down a side street. They broke away from the solid mass of wagons and people and headed through an alley into another quieter street. Dāvids—who was driving the wagon—followed closely. He had never been in Liepaja before, but Oskars had grown up here and was familiar with all its twisting cobblestone back streets. Valdis, now driving Māmiņa's wagon, followed behind.

Suddenly the air raid sirens wailed. Dāvids looked around in panic—where to hide? But there was no hiding place. Oskars's wagon ahead careened wildly as he cracked the whip over his horse, heading in the direction of the port. Daila clung desperately to the seat.

"Follow him!" Peter barked.

Working the whip above Melnis, Dāvids raced after Oskars, and behind him he could hear Valdis yelling at Māmiņa's horse.

Above the din of sirens, train whistles, and car horns all sounding alarms, he heard the drone of planes. He didn't dare turn around to look. "Hold onto me tight!" he yelled at Kārlis, who immediately put a strangle hold around him.

Suddenly the planes were overhead—a hellish noise that reverberated against the buildings of the narrow streets. After that, it was an experience too vast to comprehend—the scream of bombs, then the exploding, of sheets of red and yellow flames shooting skyward, of the gunshot sound of breaking glass, of screams, of the incessant roar of planes coming in wave after wave. Thick black smoke and clouds of dust burned the lungs.

Stiff with terror, Dāvids followed the wagon ahead of him. There was no safe place to hide. One house, one street, one corner was as fatal as the next. All around, people ran screaming. One man dashed in front of Dāvids's wagon.

"Watch out!" Peter bellowed.

But there was no stopping Melnis, and with his blood going cold, Dāvids heard the man scream as the wagon wheel rolled over him, then again as Valdis's wagon crushed him.

Ahead of him he saw a tall-spired church explode in flames, and the ground rocked when a bomb blasted a pole in an open park. Gutted buildings, dead bodies, and clogging rubble flashed before him in a sickening blur.

The waves of droning, roaring planes passed, but the crackle of flames made the scene a nightmare. Finally Oskars turned a corner. Far ahead Dāvids could see the tall steel arms of cranes—the shipyard! They were nearing the port. Ahead of them a straggly column of Nazi soldiers made their way toward the ships—probably one of the last troops to get out, Dāvids thought grimly.

Oskars slowed his wagon, picking his way through rubble, and the others did likewise. Suddenly from somewhere in the smoke-choked sky above them they heard the whine of more bombs.

"Dāvid!" came a startled cry from somewhere, but the screaming sound of bombs drowned out any other words. Before Dāvids could look around, an explosion rocketed him off the wagon, and he slammed against a wall as debris rained down on him. Numbly he looked at his brother, whose arms—paralyzed in terror—were still locked around him.

"Elita!" A scream pierced his fogged consciousness, and he pried off Kārlis's arms. "Elita!" It was Oskars, and the anguish in his voice told Dāvids, even before he saw it, that his mother's wagon had been hit.

Leaping free of his brother, he raced to where her horse lay writhing in a pool of blood. Oskars had already reached his mother, and he sat beside her, cradling her in his arms. It was clear she was dead, and her blood flowed over his trousers.

"Elita—my beloved!" he sobbed, crushing her body to him. "Why couldn't it have been me? Oh God, my Elita—why?" He buried his face in her disheveled blond hair.

In the face of Oskars's grief, Dāvids could only stare, feeling nothing. Then he heard a strangled sob behind him.

"Valdis—where is he?" Daila said in a voice vague with shock. She moved around woodenly, lifting a board as though expecting to find him hiding under it. Then Dāvids saw the body—or part of it—hurled atop a pile of rubble.

Peter, blood streaming down his face, saw the body, too. Quickly he turned and embraced Daila, leading her away. "He's dead," he said gently. "Don't search anymore. It's too ugly. But he's dead—I saw him. Go to Kārlis—he's scared—he's crying—he needs you."

Numbly Daila moved to the sobbing boy, and Dāvids turned back to the bombed wagon. There was no sign of Rolfs or Marta—just parts of bodies and the smell of burning flesh. The wagon was splintered.

"Dāvid!" the unknown voice exclaimed, and moving numbly, Dāvids turned to see Friedrich leaping over rubble, coming toward him. Vaguely he wondered if the man had been part of the column of soldiers ahead of them. "Are you all right?" Friedrich asked, his eyes going quickly over Dāvids.

With tear-filled eyes, Dāvids nodded toward Māmiņa's blood-soaked body still cradled in Oskars's arms. "My mother," he sobbed. "They killed her." He didn't even know whether it was a German or a Russian plane that dropped the bomb. It didn't matter. Nothing mattered. Nothing.

A shiver ran through Friedrich, as though the death of Dāvids's mother was as tragic to him as the death of his own mother.

"Come," the Nazi murmured. "Get to the boats. Save the rest of your family."

Dāvids nodded and tugged at his godfather's sleeve. "Come—we can't stay here."

"She's dead," Oskars murmured in a grief-choked voice, and the tear-stained face he turned up was that of an old, old man—haggard, lined with sorrow. One lens in his eyeglasses had been cracked. "Why couldn't it have been me?"

There was no answer to the anguished cry.

Friedrich gently lifted Māmiņa's body and placed it in Oskars's wagon, covering it with a blanket, while Peter, his arm in its sling, watched silently, tears in his eyes. Though he had seen Māmiņa's mental deterioration, it was clear he felt deep compassion for her, and her brutal death had hit him hard. Knowing this made Dāvids love this silent Russian man even more.

Oskars—moving stiffly—climbed in and sat beside Māmiņa's body. Dāvids glanced over at Daila, holding Kārlis in her arms. Her hands moved automatically, patting his shoulder as she crooned to him. But her eyes stared vacantly.

"Peter," Dāvids cried out in desperation, "what'll happen to her? Will she—?" he swallowed hard. "Will she become like Māmiņa?"

"No," came the deep-voiced reply. "Not Daila. She's in shock right now—it's natural. So is Oskars. But Daila's like Jānis Ozols—strong. She won't break. Kārlis needs her—and she'll come through." Peter pulled out a handkerchief and wiped the blood on his face, wincing as he exposed a deep cut on his forehead. "You take her and Kārlis in your wagon. I'll drive Oskars's wagon."

Somehow Dāvids got Daila and Kārlis into his wagon. Then, numb still with shock, he climbed up, but his hands couldn't seem to move, to grasp the reins. Friedrich leaped up beside him, flicked the reins, and they followed Peter driving Oskars's wagon ahead, going toward the port.

"The prison," Dāvids asked, "what happened to the men?"

"I left a couple of weeks ago," Friedrich replied. "I heard it was blown off the face of the earth."

Dāvids couldn't even feel satisfaction that Comrade Shimkevich had finally paid the penalty for his terrible brutality. Tears made trails down his dust-covered face as he watched Oskars gently touch Māmiņa's blood-stained blond hair. A moment ago there had been nine of them. Now there were only five. How many of them would actually reach Germany?

CHAPTER 14

THE LITTLE group arrived at the port of Liepaja in late afternoon, to a scene of utter chaos. Flames licked greedily at a gutted building as fire engines fought a losing battle to contain the blaze. The steel crane Dāvids had seen earlier was twisted grotesquely, and in the harbor a ship burned. Wagons and people were everywhere—total confusion.

At the far end of the port a ragged column of German soldiers filed aboard a submarine. Other soldiers, carrying rifles with bayonets attached, held off refugees desperately trying to get aboard. Another column of soldiers—the ones Dāvids had seen ahead of them earlier—waited to go aboard.

Dāvids looked around, confused by the tumult. Never in his life had he seen a sight like the havoc, the hysteria, and the pandemonium here at this port. It was beyond his ability to grasp it all, and he moved robotlike. Behind him in the wagon Kārlis hiccupped in fright.

The port itself was a long dock, and behind the dock

was a large plaza, or square, surrounded by old brick buildings. One end of this square had already been damaged, but as they inched their way through the crowd, following the endless line of refugees and their wagons, Dāvids saw that the far end was still comparatively intact. Here and there long lines of people queued up, while men yelled orders.

In the harbor an endless array of ships were moored—big, little, old and new, some delapidated floating tubs covered with rust, others reasonably trim and well-tended. There was the submarine being loaded and several military ships jammed with troops already sailing out of the harbor.

Dāvids looked around, wondering how to get on one of those ships at the dock.

"Over there," Friedrich said, pointing to a stall-like structure at the end of the main dock. "Get a pass to go aboard a boat." He jumped down and extended his hand. "I must get back to my unit. Maybe our paths will cross again, my friend. Till then, *auf Wiedersehen*."

"Where will you go?" Dāvids asked, taking the offered hand.

Friedrich nodded to the troops waiting to board the submarine. "We return to Germany." Quickly he dashed across the crowded pier and was soon lost in the mass of humanity.

"Stay with the wagon," Dāvids yelled over the noise to Daila; then he leaped down and hurried to join one of the lines. All around were many such lines, all leading to stall-like structures, where people fought to get passage of some sort. As he watched, he realized there was no set manner of getting passes. In the chaotic commotion, almost anything happened as the authorities tried to funnel the refugees onto ships.

So Dāvids waited, his eyes streaming tears, partly due to exhaustion, sorrow, shock, and the black smoke that permeated the area. He wanted to cry, to cry for hours until he could wash away the lump that almost choked him. The tears running down his grimy face did nothing to ease the pain. They were superficial tears. The hurt inside was too deep, too painful to surface.

Finally Peter joined him, handing him the passports for Daila, Kārlis, and Oskars.

"I made arrangements for your mother to be buried," he said simply.

Dāvids nodded. He knew she would be interred in one of the many mass graves.

When his turn came, it was almost dark, and he handed the man in the stall his passports, including Peter's.

"Where are the others?" the sweat-smelling man asked, wiping a river of perspiration off his smoke-grimed face as he peered out into the dusk. Dāvids pointed to Oskars, Daila, and Kārlis huddled miserably in the two wagons.

"How're you going to pay for your permits?" the man asked.

Reluctant to part with the German marks in his money belt quite so soon, Dāvids merely shrugged.

"You got any food?" the man asked.

"Yes—some—some bacon."

"Any sugar?"

"No—but I have a little honey."

"I'll take a side of bacon and four liters of honey."

Dāvids looked into the stall. Piled up inside were all sorts of food items—household items and various bags —anything a scared, desperate refugee would pay for a permit. He didn't blame the guy. It was hell—trying to live. Possessions now had only one value—how far could it get you from here?

Peter hurried to get the honey and bacon and in a few minutes Dāvids had his permit—it was that simple. No questions—no proof of ownership of the passports. In fact, the man had scarcely looked at them. Dāvids had a hunch that even without passports, permits could be gotten if one was willing to pay the price.

"What boat do we get on?" he asked.

Again the man mopped his face. "All the boats are full. You've got to wait—maybe tomorrow. Hang onto your permits. Now move on—I've got others to take care of." He motioned Dāvids away.

By the light of the distant burning building, Dāvids and Peter made their way back to their wagons. Daila made no comment when told they would remain in Liepaja overnight. Still moving dully, she spread blankets out in the wagon bed, and after giving Kārlis a chunk of bread to eat, she tucked him in, crooning softly to him until he fell asleep. The two wagons were parked side by side, and Oskars lay down in his own wagon. Dāvids, wanting to comfort his heartbroken godfather, lay down beside him.

"My boy—my dear Dāvid," Oskars murmured after a while, as his arm folded over Dāvids. "You're all I have left." There was a long silence, then Oskars continued. "How well I remember that day you were born—how honored I was when Jānis and Elita told me they had named you Dāvids Oskars—and I would be your godfather. Such an honor—so great an honor," came the soft, dreamy voice. "And how pleased Elita looked! Ah, my beloved Elita!" He gave a dry sob and said no more. Soon he slept, while Dāvids thought back to all the times he and Oskars had done things together. They had both loved fishing, and for hours they'd sat beside a river, saying little, content to be sharing something. With aching heart he yearned for the peaceful days, when their biggest worry was whether or not they caught a fish.

Sometime during the night he woke to hear Daila sobbing. He saw Peter take her in his arms and croon to her, even as she had crooned to Kārlis earlier, until she had cried all the heartache and misery out of her soul. Dāvids ached to be able to do the same—but no tears came.

He slept intermittently, and at dawn the port seemed little changed. Some ships were gone, but in their place were others. Already lines were formed in front of the stalls and bleary-eyed, calloused men issued permits while their pile of loot grew larger.

Dāvids saw one ship that was just being moored and the line in front of it was quite short. Quickly they drove their wagons over in place. The ship was large—a rusting, paint-peeling old one, but it looked stout.

Before leaving his wagon to get in line, he glanced back to Daila, worried about her. She had suffered a terrible loss. But the determination in her eyes told him she had put her pain behind her. She would carry on.

Relieved, he spoke to the leathery, skinny man who stood beside the gangplank. "We want passage. There are five of us."

The man looked them over carefully, then his eyes greedily scanned the sturdy wagons and the healthy horses.

"You can't take wagons and animals aboard—no room—"

"But I saw animals and wagons going aboard yesterday," Dāvids argued hotly. He pointed to a ship at the far end of the dock, where a wagon was being pulled up a wide ramp into the hold opening. "See—they're taking wagons."

The man shrugged. "That's them. You want to take your wagon—you go over there. We don't have that kind of hold." He gave a thin-lipped smile. "But by the time you get over there, they'll be full up."

"The boats are filling fast, Dāvid," Peter said quietly beside him. "We're here—we'd better take passage while we can."

"But Melnis—" Dāvids wailed.

"Better to give up Melnis than risk your whole family."

With a sigh so deep that it came from his innermost tormented soul, Dāvids nodded.

"Load all your stuff aboard," the leathery man said, "then come back here and bring your certificates for the horses."

Everything was carried aboard the ship. "Daila, you and Kārlis stay here," Dāvids said in a flat voice. "Peter and I will go down and finish up the details."

"I'll go, too," Oskars said. "I've got to sign the paper for my own horse." Oskars seemed to have buried his heartache and moved with a steady stride. Only his pale eyes behind the cracked glasses showed his inner misery.

A long line of weary, frightened refugees, most carrying their meager possessions in bundles, streamed steadily aboard the ship. The port and its big plaza teemed with humanity. The Russian army was closing in fast, and the mass of people desperately sought passage out of Latvia. A lone plane overhead caused panic, and the noise and confusion was deafening. Finally it flew away. But it was only a matter of time—a day or two at the most—and Liepaja's harbor would be totally destroyed, thereby cutting off the exodus. This knowledge was written clearly on every desperate face.

"See that baldheaded guy?" the man at the gangplank said when the three of them came down to give him their papers. He pointed to a reedy, chisel-faced man some distance away, standing beside a makeshift stall. "Go give them to him. He's taking care of everything for me. I'm too busy." He waved them off and turned to another refugee waiting to go aboard.

Dāvids led his horse and wagon through the mob, toward the man who would take possession. When he stopped he couldn't bear the thought of giving up his horse. Wrapping his arms around Melnis's neck, he let the tears flow over the sleek black hair. In giving up the horse he had worked so hard to buy, it seemed as though he was giving up his last link to Latvia. He sobbed for Māmiņa, who had never really lived after Papus was gone; for Valdis, who died inwardly the day Jēkabs was shot; and for Marta and Rolfs, who were almost like family. He cried for Stulbenis, who was dumb but not so dumb that he couldn't pull a boy out of a frozen pond. Lastly his tears were for Yuri and Adrei, who wanted to be farmers; and for Friedrich, who might return someday to live peacefully with his family.

Finally the pain in his heart eased and he dried his eyes. Then he turned to the baldheaded man. Latvia and his heartache were behind him.

To his surprise, the man and Oskars were warmly shaking hands and embracing one another as old friends. Peter stood stoically aside, as though patiently waiting for the sentimental little man and the tearful boy to get their emotions under control. Dāvids gave a weak, sheepish grin, and to his amazement Peter's hard face softened in a smile of understanding.

Oskars turned and pulled Dāvids toward him. "My boy, meet my dear friend, Vilmārs. He's known your

father and me since we were boys. Vilmār," he added
proudly, "this is my godson, Dāvids Ozols."

Solemnly Dāvids put out his hand and Vilmārs grasped
it excitedly, his eyes bright. "Jānis's boy? God be praised!"
He shook the hand vigorously. "My boy, Jānis is searching
frantically for you—"

"Jānis—alive?" Oskars gasped. "Here?"

"Where *is* Papus?" Dāvids practically yelled in heart-
pounding excitement. "Where is he? Tell me!" Peter
crowded in beside them, instantly alert.

"Somewhere here in Liepaja," Vilmārs said eagerly.
"Around the port someplace. He's been combing the area
for a week—figuring you'd be coming through here."

"He—he wanders *free* here?" Peter asked.

Vilmārs laughed dryly, waving a hand over the
pressing mob. "Everybody here is too busy looking after
his own hide to bother with anyone else. Besides, these
refugees have had all they can stomach of the Gestapo
and NKVD. No policeman would dare venture into this
mob to arrest a man. He'd be stampeded. There are
probably a lot of men like Jānis here, running free,
searching for family."

Oskars looked from Peter to Dāvids, then back to
Peter, his eyes puzzled. "You knew he was alive?" he
asked numbly. "How?"

Peter didn't bother to answer. "Let's go find him," he
said instead. "I'll cover the far end." To Oskars he added
gruffly, "You search by those brick buildings. Dāvid, you
scour the wharf area. Whoever finds him, get back to the
ship, stand aboard, and wave something—a shirt, a kerchief—anything for a flag." Immediately Peter disappeared into the crowd.

With a grin of pure joy spreading across his face,
Dāvids, too, went searching. Frantically he looked, curs-

ing his short stature. Finally he climbed up on someone's wagon to peer over the pressing mob—but in such a crowd, how could he ever find a man who was not very tall himself? He could see Peter moving relentlessly toward the distant end of the port, his dark head turning from side to side.

For an hour he searched, constantly glancing toward the ship, hoping to see the signal.

Suddenly the ear-splitting wail of sirens pierced the air, and people dashed about frantically, driven by mass hysteria to find shelter. Dāvids was caught in the crush. He knew if he stumbled, he'd be trampled to death. Pushed along by a wave of humanity, he reached out for a wagon wheel and dragged himself under the wagon where two women and a baby sat huddled in terror. All around him the pounding feet and screaming voices made a thunderous roar that all but drowned out the throbbing sound of low-flying bombers.

Somehow the mass of humanity disappeared, swallowed up in the many side streets opening onto the plaza, leaving only a few hundred people trying to find safety. He saw Peter standing next to a concrete abutment by the pier, turning his head, constantly searching. And Oskars was running toward a side street. He, too, seemed to be looking even as he scurried along.

Suddenly, coming out of one of the red brick buildings facing the plaza was a familiar figure.

"Papu!" Dāvids bellowed with all his might. "Papu! Over here!" Oblivious to the deafening sound of planes, he leaped out from under the wagon, waving his arms and screaming.

Oskars stopped in his tracks and spun around at the sound of Dāvids's cry, and at the same time Papus heard

Dāvids and dashed forward. Oskars saw Jānis Ozols and headed toward his friend—arms outstretched.

So intent was Dāvids on reaching his father that he didn't hear the screaming whistle of bombs. He saw Oskars throw himself at Papus, and he knew no more.

When he came to, he was lying under a pile of debris, his head throbbing. He didn't know where he was. Then it all came back, and with frantic strength, he tossed the debris off and scrambled to his feet.

The sight before him almost stopped his heart. The once beautiful ancient red brick buildings were in flames, their wooden interiors burning fast. The harbor square, surrounded by the burning buildings, was a scene of wanton destruction. Dead bodies were everywhere, and the injured wailed and screamed in pain.

Dazed, Dāvids maneuvered around gaping holes, heading to where he had seen Papus last. He didn't dare hope—or think. Finally he saw Oskars sprawled on the ground, blood pouring from a gaping hole in his back. Beneath him was Papus!

Gently he rolled Oskars over and heard him moan. He was alive! Then Dāvids bent his head and placed it against Papus's chest—overwhelmed with relief when he heard a heartbeat.

"Oh dear God—forgive me," Oskars murmured through bloodless lips.

Gently Dāvids touched his face. The glasses were gone, but Oskars didn't need them. His eyes were closed. "You never did anything that needed forgiving, Oskar," he said gently.

"I betrayed him," Oskars murmured, breathing in shallow gasps.

"Betrayed whom?" But even as Dāvids asked the

question, he felt as though a hand had closed over his heart, wringing the life out of it. Everything in him screamed, "No, don't let him say it! No!"

"I told the NKVD—about his hidden guns."

Dāvids felt leaden. It couldn't be true. Not devoted, loyal Oskars. He tried to speak, but the lump in his throat choked off the words. So great was his shock that he couldn't feel hate. He couldn't feel a thing.

The weak, gasping voice continued, while the eyes remained closed. "They suspected—wanted to know more—like where he got them—where he delivered—so they arrested me—his close friend." A sob tore out of Oskars. "Beat me—broke my arm—I wouldn't talk. More than once I was beaten—" A shudder of remembering shook his frail body. "Those beasts—animals—they knew I'd never tell—but they knew my weakness." Oskars's voice faded, and he seemed scarcely to breathe. "They made me watch—through a grating—they beat my dear Dāvids. Asked him silly questions—but they beat him." Another shudder wracked his body. "I couldn't let them—they would've killed him—killed my Dāvids. I—I broke down—promised I would tell—if—if they—released him—" Tears spilled out from behind the closed eyes and dribbled down the lined face. "Oh, my God—Jāni—I betrayed you—" He gave a convulsive shudder and his head rolled to one side as his mouth hung loose. Oskars Mitulis was dead.

Dāvids sat staring with tears running down his grimy face. He remembered the suffering on Oskars's face the day after Papus was taken away, the pain in his voice when he said, "He was my friend, Dāvid—my dear, dear friend. Oh, God—how I hate them!" Then the indignation when he'd seen Peter on the farm and he'd declared, "A Bolshevik on Jānis's farm—it's immoral—disgraceful!" And when Māmiņa had died, he had sobbed, "Why couldn't it have been me?" Oskars had sworn before God always to protect the child who bore his name, and he had fulfilled that oath at a terrible cost to himself. Life for Oskars had been a living death. Now it was over.

All around, soldiers were giving first aid to the injured and removing the dead. And the refugees were streaming back into the port area.

Papus groaned and stirred, blinking his eyes as he tried to focus on Dāvids. Gone was his flowing mustache, but there was no disguising the white scar, the square jaw, or the stocky frame. The hazel eyes that once crinkled with laughter now looked at his son, telling of torture and hunger and loneliness. The war had left its mark on him, as it had on them all.

"My boy, I've found you at last," Papus said thickly as he struggled to sit up. Dāvids, overcome with sorrow for Oskars and joy in finding his father, embraced him and buried his face in his neck. "Oh, Papu—it's really you," he murmured.

"The family—?" Papus asked when Dāvids released him and helped him to his feet. "Are they safe?"

Quickly Dāvids glanced toward the ship. In the confusion he'd forgotten about them. But the ship was undamaged. "Daila and Kārlis—yes."

"And your mother?"

Dāvids looked back at him sadly. "She—she—a bomb killed her, Papu. Valdis, too—and Marta and Rolf—hit their wagon. And Oskars—he just died."

Papus lowered his head. "My poor little Elita," he murmured, and a sob wracked his body. Then he wiped an arm across his face and looked down at Oskars by their feet. "And now my old friend." Tears filled his eyes. "He gave his life for me, Dāvid." He knelt beside the body and touched the thin-lined face. "Good-bye, my friend. Thank you for years of love and loyalty."

Dāvids turned away. Evidently Papus had never been told who had betrayed him. He still believed it was his son.

Papus rose and slid an arm across his son's shoulder. "I'm glad you were with him at the end. He loved you so." He gave a sad smile. "For you he would have done anything."

"I know," Dāvids murmured. For him Oskars had betrayed his lifelong friend.

Two soldiers came up and paused. "I'm sorry," one man said, "but we've got to take the body."

Papus nodded.

"Wait!" Dāvids spoke up, and he reached down into Oskars's pocket and removed the permit for boarding the ship. Handing it to Papus, he added, "This will get you aboard."

Then the men carried Oskars's body away.

As they turned to head toward the ship, they saw Peter hobbling toward them, blood streaming down one leg, but otherwise he was unharmed by the bombing.

"Peter!" Papus cried out in joyful surprise, and eagerly he clasped his hands. "Oh, I'm so glad you made it here."

Silently Peter grasped his hands. "We'd better hurry," he said, "the ship will be leaving soon."

Quickly the three dashed to the distant gangplank.

Hours later, the group stood on the ship's crowded dock as it pulled out of the harbor. Papus had one arm around Daila and the other around Kārlis as he faced Dāvids and Peter. He had told them very briefly of his escape, the months of hiding in Smolensk, in the

Ukraine, and finally his flight into Poland. When he'd heard of Latvia's impending fall into Russian hands again, he risked returning to the port, staying with Vilmārs, while he searched among the refugees for his family.

"Papu, who betrayed you? How many people knew you were smuggling guns?" Daila asked finally in a low voice. This was the question that haunted Dāvids, and he held his breath—waiting.

"Very few—Oskars, Peter—and a man named Alfreds, to whom I delivered the guns," Papus replied. "Alfreds was killed outright, and no amount of torture could have made any of the others betray me." He stared at the still burning harbor, his face sad. "I think the NKVD *suspected* me but never could prove anything. So they finally got me on a mere technicality—something unimportant—" His voice trailed off.

The misery within Dāvids turned into a leaden weight. Papus still believed that his own son—in a moment of weakness—had confessed something, maybe about the hidden black-market food—and on this he was arrested. True, Papus felt it unimportant perhaps, and he had no doubt long ago forgiven his son for this supposed weakness. But the thought was there.

Every nerve in him wanted to cry out, "But it wasn't me, Papu! I didn't tell. My only confession was admitting we had a radio. I'm innocent, Papu. I'm innocent. It was Oskars—not me." But the words wouldn't come.

He turned away—and found himself looking into Peter's dark eyes, and he knew that Peter *did* know who had done it. Evidently the NKVD official—Comrade Vladimirov—had told him. But in Peter's eyes he saw the message—better that Papus think a child weakened under torture and confessed some trivial thing than to believe his friend had deliberately betrayed him. This was easier to accept—easier to forgive.

Dāvids looked away. Someday he would tell Peter why Oskars had done it. It seemed important that Oskars not be condemned.

"Will we ever come back to Latvia?" Daila asked as the blazing harbor grew farther and farther away.

"Maybe," Papus replied softly. "If the British or Americans demand that Russia give up occupation of the Baltics at the end of the war."

"Russia gives up nothing," Peter murmured bitterly. "Russia takes."

"What happens to us, then?" Kārlis asked.

"We've been through hell and survived," Papus replied. "We're together now. We've made the best of every situation, and we will in the future. Even if we have to go live in a foreign country."

"Peter, too?" Dāvids asked.

Papus smiled, having been told about Peter's forged passport. "Certainly. He's family."

Peter gave a sheepish grin, and Dāvids knew he was pleased. Peter had been alone too long. He needed to belong to someone. And remembering the night on the pier when Peter consoled a heartbroken Daila, he secretly hoped that someday Peter might become his legal brother-in-law.

Late that evening, as the ship sailed close to shore, hoping to avoid being seen by Russian bombers as it headed toward the German Baltic coast, Kārlis sat on a corner of the deck sketching the sunset. Slowly he drew the Latvian crimson-white-crimson flag superimposed over the sunset.

"What's that mean?" Dāvids asked him.

"It depicts the sunset of freedom for Latvia," Kārlis answered in a sad voice. "The blackness of Soviet imperialism is swallowing it."

Dāvids looked at the faces around him—at Papus, Daila, Peter, and the many refugees crowded on the deck. In their faces he saw resistance to such an idea.

"Just remember this, Kārli," he said firmly. "Where there's a sunset, there will be a sunrise. Latvia has been occupied many, many times. But she won her independence. And someday she will again see her sunrise—be free again."

Papus smiled at him, and in that smile Dāvids saw pride—a pride that erased any disappointment Papus might have had that he lacked the ability to resist. He knew he had been forgiven. He looked out across the orange-tinted sea. Now he would make a new life—one free from guilt.

Softly someone started singing a hauntingly sad song, and one by one others joined in. Soon the sad song ended, and then as the last rays of twilight touched the fading shore of their beloved homeland, the refugees raised their voices as if on cue, and the lilting music of their national anthem rang out over the waters of the Baltic Sea. It was as though they wanted the waves to take back the message that someday the war would end, and there would be sunrise again in Latvia, and they would return.

EPILOGUE

AFTER THE END of the war in May 1945, Latvian underground soldiers fled to the western province of Kurzeme, where they put up a stiff resistance to the Red army, hoping to prove to the American and British governments that Latvians did not want to be part of the Soviet Union. They hoped to force the governments into demanding that they be set free. But their efforts were in vain.

Freedom for Latvia and her sister Baltic countries gave way to oppressive occupation. The thousands of refugees who fled to Germany were put in displaced persons camps, and eventually they found their way to England, Australia, America, and to almost every part of the world. But in their hearts there remains the hope that someday freedom will come again for Latvia.